DIANE STANLEY

THE MYSTERIOUS MATTER OF I. M. FINE

HarperTrophy®
An Imprint of HarperCollinsPublishers

The Mysterious Matter of I. M. Fine
Copyright © 2001 by Diane Stanley
All rights reserved. No part of this book may be used or reproduced in any manner
whatsoever without written permission except in the case of brief quotations
embodied in critical articles and reviews. Printed in the United States of America.
For information address HarperCollins Children's Books, a division of
HarperCollins Publishers, 1350 Avenue of the Americas, New York, NY 10019.

Library of Congress Cataloging-in-Publication Data
Stanley, Diane.
    The mysterious matter of I. M. Fine / by Diane Stanley.
        p.   cm.
    Summary: Noticing that a popular series of horror novels is having a bizarre
effect on the behavior of its readers, Franny and Beamer set out to find the
mysterious author.
    ISBN 0-688-17546-5 — ISBN 0-06-029619-4 (lib. bdg.)
    ISBN 0-380-73327-7 (pbk.)
    [1. Magic—Fiction. 2. Books and reading—Fiction. 3. Mystery and
detective stories.]   I. Title.
PZ7.S7869 My   2001   00-054040
[Fic]—dc21   CIP
                                                             AC

Book design by Andrea Vandergrift
❖
First Harper Trophy edition, 2002

Visit us on the World Wide Web!
www.harperchildrens.com

~

For Elaine Scott

1

A few years ago, I made up a game to play with the packing boxes. It was called Find the Treasure. The twins and I would pick something familiar—like the eggbeater, say, or the candlesticks—and that would be the treasure. Then while Mom and Dad were unpacking things and putting them away, we would start madly opening boxes, trying to find it. Whoever found the treasure first got to pick the coolest bedroom in the new house. Of course, since Mom and Dad were under the impression that we were actually helping them unpack, they expected us to do things like take the dishes into the kitchen—not just pile them on the floor and move on to the next box. This provided an added challenge.

The last time we moved, the idea just popped into

my head that it would be a lot more exciting if, instead of a treasure, it was a bomb—and if we didn't find it in time, the whole house would blow up! We got so frenzied trying to save the family from annihilation that we broke a couple of things and our parents got really annoyed.

After that, we quit playing the game and just helped unpack like normal kids (normal kids, that is, who move a lot).

Still, the idea of a time bomb hidden among the packing boxes, with their innocent labels (KITCHEN, BED LINENS, TOYS), haunted me.

Later, after everything that happened, I remembered the game and wondered what had put the idea into my head, and why it had stayed with me so stubbornly. It was almost as if I somehow knew, way back then, what was going to happen.

Now, I know this sounds really mystical and off-the-wall, and I apologize about that. And, of course, if you want to be absolutely literal about it, the whole I. M. Fine thing wasn't about bombs at all. But once you've read this story, I think you'll understand. It was just a different kind of time bomb in a different kind of package. But it was every bit as dangerous as the real thing. And just like in the game, time was running out.

Well, you'll see.

2

First, I should explain about the moving.

My father is a consultant to community colleges. Once, he actually started a new school from scratch, and that took several years. But usually he just helps reorganize their programs. Either way, once he gets things whipped into shape, we move on.

My mom works, too, but moving isn't a problem for her. Her job is translating books and articles from German into English, which she does out of a home office. She must be really psyched about the fact that she can take her work with her wherever she goes, because she mentions it a lot.

As for me and Zoë and J.D.—well, apparently they think that all we really need—besides loving parents, of course—are a house to live in and a school to go to. I guess when you get older, you kind of forget what it's like to start all over in a new school with a bunch of kids who have known one another since they were playing with blocks back in preschool.

We complain about it every time we have to move. In response, we get a sigh and a lecture, which never fails to cover the following four points. One: Dad has to go where the work is. (Usually, they follow this with a reminder that the money he makes helps put food on our table, like we hadn't figured that out already. Also, this is supposed to make us feel guilty for complaining.) Two: My Mom grew up in a navy family. They moved all the time, and she turned out just fine. Three: Think how lucky we are to have been so many different places! And four: Think of it as a challenge!

That last one is easier said than done. Of the three of us, my sister, Zoë, is the only one who can really operate that way. Not that she likes starting over every year—she just doesn't let it stop her. Every time she arrives at a new school, she's like a kid on a mission, determined to make friends or die trying. Though she's only ten, Zoë has developed some kind of inner radar that allows her to figure out everything you need to know to be popular. First day at a new school, she comes home with a whole new vocabulary. Plus, she has to go shopping right away because everybody is wearing pop-beads or socks with cats on them and she has to wear them, too.

Within three weeks, Zoë will have been invited to a party or at least to spend the night at someone's house. It's a real talent. I wish I had it.

J.D., my little brother, is Zoë's twin. I used to think he was kind of an "anti-Zoë," that he just looked to see what she was doing and then did the opposite. But after I thought about it some more, I decided that wasn't fair to J.D. He just has his own special outlook on life. He doesn't seem to care whether the other kids like him or not. He's glad if they do, but he's not willing to reinvent himself to fit in. And oddly enough, he usually fits in just fine.

Since J.D. is likely to do or say almost anything that occurs to him at the moment, he sometimes gets labeled the class clown. But that makes him sound like one of those needy types who are always looking for attention—which he isn't. He's a happy kid who just rolls along and takes things as they come. That's a real talent, too.

And me? My approach to making friends is to hide in plain sight until somebody finds me. I guess I'd better explain.

It started because I like to read so much. I will read anything: I read the stuff on the back of cereal boxes at breakfast. I read the billboards when we're driving in the car. I will even read *Popular Mechanics* or *Florida Real Estate Monthly* if that's all they have in the dentist's waiting room. Of course, I'd rather read a good book, so most of the time I have one with me, just in case I have a spare moment with nothing to do.

It didn't take me long to discover that having a book with you at all times can come in handy in other situations besides long waits in doctors' offices and airport lounges. Like, for example, those embarrassing times when you're sitting alone in the lunchroom, surrounded by about a million complete strangers who all know one another and are chatting away and having a great time that doesn't include you. All you have to do is open your book. Suddenly, you don't look pathetic anymore. Plus, you're reading something interesting, so pretty soon you forget where you are and it doesn't matter that you don't have anyone to talk to.

A book is like a little room you can carry around with you, and anytime you need to, you can slip in there to get away from it all. So that's the hiding part.

But, of course, a book is not really a room. You are standing there—or sitting there—in plain sight. And eventually, somebody is bound to come over and talk to you. Usually, they ask what you're reading. So you put down your book and smile and start telling them about it—and before you know it, you've made a new friend. I'll admit that's a kind of wimpy way of going about it, but it works.

A year ago last summer, we moved to Baltimore, or rather, to a suburb outside of Baltimore. We hit the ground running, since we had only two weeks till school started, and we had a lot to do.

The first order of business was to get the above-mentioned boxes unpacked and the furniture arranged and the pictures on the walls and the books on the shelves and food in the kitchen. While we were doing all that, the cable guy and the meter reader and the telephone man all showed up and did what they usually do. Finally, when the house was reasonably livable, we moved on to phase two.

This involved going to our new dentist to get our teeth cleaned and to our new pediatrician for checkups and shots. All five of us got haircuts. Then Mom took us over to the school to get us registered and then to the office-supply store for notebooks and binders and college-ruled paper and then, last but not least, to the mall to buy clothes. Amazingly, we got it all done.

Two days later, school started.

Now, the first day of school is majorly important if you're the new kid. People tend to notice you and size you up, so if on that day you develop a huge, disgusting pimple or you say something really stupid, or your most recent haircut was kind of unfortunate—well, it takes a long time to undo the damage. I always go out of my way to look as good as I can.

I put on my new outfit, which we had bought at the mall only two days before and which was probably the coolest outfit I'd ever had. The top was this buttery yellow T-shirt with rainbow trim around the neck and sleeves. It went with a white denim skirt with the same trim on the pockets. It fit perfectly, and Mom said the yellow shirt brought out the golden highlights in my hair. So I figured I was making a pretty good impression.

Of course, this checking-out business swings both ways. While they were looking me over, I was busy sizing up the school, the kids, and the teacher. And on the whole, my conclusion was that Park Place Intermediate was pretty ordinary. This is a good thing, in case you're wondering. No big surprises. No weird customs. I like it that way.

The only thing that was in any way remarkable was my teacher, Mrs. Lamb. Though she was probably older than my mother, she looked like she had just stepped off the cover of a romance novel, with this wild mass of curly red hair and peachy pale skin and bright blue eyes. She wore flowing silk dresses in colorful prints and had a deep, throaty voice. And she had more pep than the Energizer bunny. Like I said, she was not ordinary at all—but everything else was.

In mid-September, we had a string of gusty, rainy days. The lunchroom was really crowded, since nobody could eat outside in the rain. The only empty seats I could find were at the end of the table where DeeDee Sanderson and her pals were sitting.

Now DeeDee is not my favorite person, even though she is the most popular girl in the class—maybe in the whole sixth grade. Why she's so popular, I can't imagine. I'll admit that she's really pretty and has cool clothes and great hair. But the popular girls I've known in the past are usually nice to everybody, which is part of why they're popular. Not DeeDee.

Let me just give you one example. During the second week of school, DeeDee and her little group passed me in the hall. She gave me this sideways look, then started giggling and whispering to her friends.

"What?" I said. Did I have a Rice Krispie stuck to my nose or something?

DeeDee smirked. "You must really like that" is what she said. She sort of glanced down at my clothes—my new outfit with the rainbow trim. "'Cause this is like the fourth time you've worn it since school started."

After that, every time I opened my closet and reached for my new outfit, I got this sick, embarrassed feeling and picked something else instead. I even started keeping a list of what I wore each day so I wouldn't repeat an outfit more than every two weeks—which wasn't all that easy, since I don't have all that many clothes. Not to mention what a stupid waste of time and energy it was.

Anyway, as you can imagine, I would have preferred to sit anyplace else on the planet besides DeeDee's table. Well, except maybe on the floor, which was my only alternative. So I took the very end seat and, doing my best to ignore her, began laying out all my stuff—my cream cheese and olive sandwich on rye, my Granny Smith apple, my brownie, my book—when someone sat down across from me. He plopped his lunch bag onto the table and ripped it open in this noisy way you couldn't possibly avoid noticing.

So I looked up, and there sat this tall kid from my class. He had longish hair and a longish nose and very dark eyes. Maybe he got his growth spurt early or maybe he's going to be a giant when he grows up, but he looked way too big for sixth grade.

He said his name was Beamer.

"Like the car?" I asked.

"The car?"

"BMW. Beemer," I said.

"Who would name their kid after a car?"

"You never know," I said defensively. "Somebody named their baby Nylon."

"Really?"

"Really."

He shook his head in amazement. "Well, it's just a nickname," he said. "My real name is Scott."

I drew a blank. "And they call you Beamer because . . ."

"Because I kind of tune out, you know, daydream a lot. My dad goes, 'Beam me up, Scotty!' Big joke. So pretty soon I'm Beamer."

"Oh," I said, wishing I had a nickname. Anything would be better than Franny, which makes me sound like somebody's grandmother.

"You know Kinko's—the copy place?" I said. "You know why they call it that?"

"Not a clue."

"The guy who started it? He has kinky hair, and

that was his nickname—'Kinko'!"

"No kidding," Beamer said. "Are you some kind of expert on strange names?"

"No. I just read it in the newspaper."

"Speaking of strange," he said, "what do you make of the worm thing?"

"'The worm thing'?" I wasn't sure I had heard him right.

"Well, yeah. Take a look." He pointed down the table to where DeeDee and her gang were giggling hysterically. But this time, they weren't giggling at me. In front of each girl was a pile of Jelly Worms—those gummy, bright-colored candies. There are also Jelly Bears and Jelly Kitties, but for some reason they only had the Worms—lots of them. They kept sliding them around on the table, making them bump into one another. Every time they did this, they squealed with laughter. They were making the worms run up their arms, putting them on their heads. One girl had even used paper clips to make Jelly Worm earrings.

"Wow," I said. "That is so weird!"

"They're all doing it," he said.

I looked from table to table. He was right. The same thing was going on at every one of them. It was like one big Jelly Worm theme party.

"This isn't some strange Baltimore thing, is it?"

"It's strange, but I don't think we can blame it on Baltimore."

"So what, then?"

"I asked you."

I shrugged my shoulders and took a bite of my sandwich.

"It's a mystery," I said.

3

Zoë got home late that night. She had spent the afternoon over at some girl's house, working on a poster for a school project, and we had already started dinner by the time she was dropped off. She came rushing through the front door, all pink-cheeked and grinning with excitement, and I naturally assumed this was because she had scored yet another social triumph. But as it turned out, I was wrong. She was all fired up because she was absolutely dying for Mom to take her to the store right after supper. Can you guess what it was she simply had to have?

Jelly Worms.

"Put it on the grocery list," Mom said. "I'll get some next time I go to the store."

"No," Zoë wailed. "I have to have them tomorrow!"

"Why on earth?" Mom asked.

"Everybody has them," Zoë said. "You wouldn't understand."

Both my mom and dad looked puzzled. They really didn't understand, and who could blame them?

"It's true," I admitted. "I saw it in the lunchroom today—all the kids were playing with Jelly Worms. It was beyond weird."

"Please!" Zoë begged. "You don't have to pay for them. I'll use my allowance."

Mom patted her hand. "Calm down, Zoë," she said. "I don't mind taking you to the store. I don't even mind buying the candy. I'm just trying to picture a whole lunchroom full of kids playing with Jelly Worms."

"It's that stupid book," said J.D., who was busy creating a starburst pattern of peas on his mountain of mashed potatoes.

"It is not stupid," Zoë snapped.

"What are you talking about?" we all said, in more or less the same voice.

"*The Worm Turns*," said J.D. "Everybody's reading it. Jelly Worms come to life and destroy Cincinnati."

"Not Cincinnati, you dope," said Zoë. "Cleveland."

"Whatever," said J.D. "I'm just saying if there're Jelly Worms in a Chillers book, it's going to be the new cool thing."

"No kidding!" said Dad. He put down his fork and gazed at J.D. like he had just proved that aliens built the pyramids. If you want my opinion, this was a lot more interest than the subject deserved.

"Is that a series of books? Chillers?"

"Uh-huh." J.D. filched a sprig of parsley from the serving platter and inserted it in the center of his starburst. He seemed pleased with the effect.

"They're children's books? A whole series of books about the same characters, like Nancy Drew?"

"No, different characters every time," Zoë said. "But they're all scary."

"Okay," said Dad, "a series of scary stories for kids. And everybody reads them?"

"Yeah," I said, surprised that my dad hadn't heard of the Chillers series before. It was in the news a lot. Every time somebody wrote an article on how my generation was going to the dogs and how it was all because of violent video games and movies and rock music, there was always some mention of Chillers.

Now, I used to read Chillers books a lot. You could always count on an exciting story that would scare the

16

poo out of you. In practically every chapter, there's something that makes you jump. At first, they're usually false alarms, so that after five or six of them, you kind of relax and think, Oh, it's just the little brother jumping out from behind the tombstone again. That's when the really bad thing happens.

So, like I said, they're totally exciting to read, only after a while, they started giving me nightmares. Plus, I got a little tired of all those monsters, ghosts, vampires, blood, gore, beheadings, and rotting corpses. I moved on to *Anne of Green Gables* and books like that, which are also exciting, but in a different way.

They must not give other kids bad dreams, though. Or maybe they do, but the kids read them anyway—I don't know. But whenever a new book in the series is due to be released, kids practically camp out in front of their neighborhood bookstores to be the first in line to buy one. The author, I. M. Fine, writes four or five books a year—which, you have to admit, is pretty impressive, speedwise—and every one of them sells about a zillion copies.

"Come on," my dad said, "don't you think it's amazing that a writer of children's books could have that kind of influence over so many kids? That he could just pick something at random—a particular brand of candy—and, simply by putting it in his story, cause a nationwide fad? And look at it from a financial standpoint: What if before he wrote that book he went out and bought stock in the Jelly Worm company? Then he scribbles off his little book, through which he controls the market forces—and makes himself a rich man!"

"Honey," Mom said, "if every kid in America is buying his books, then he's already a rich man."

"Right, okay, he probably is," Dad agreed, "but that's not the point I'm trying to make. It's his ability to influence people to buy whatever he wants that impresses me."

"Why?" Mom asked. "Advertisers do it all the time. The film industry does it. Name one recent children's movie where they didn't sell action figures and decorated lunch boxes and all kinds of toys based on the main characters. It's just capitalism in action."

"I still say this is different," Dad said, a little bit annoyed. "It's more indirect. It's more insidious. This guy isn't selling Chillers lunch boxes. He's just sitting in his office writing away, and he just happens to feature a certain brand of candy in his book—and overnight, the purchasing power of millions of children comes into play."

You could tell he was disappointed that we weren't all falling down with amazement.

"Maybe I should start reading Chillers for stock tips," Dad muttered.

Dinner was pretty much over by then. Well, except that J.D. was still eating his mashed potato mountain— very carefully, from around the edges, so as to make a scalloped design—and he was taking forever. Dad usually doesn't mind hanging around the table waiting for him to finish playing with his food, but that night Dad was really wound up. He slid his chair back, got to his feet, and, without even clearing his plate, said, "Come on, Zoë. Let's go to the store."

They were back in half an hour, both of them grinning from ear to ear. Zoë was clutching her little bag of Jelly Worms—blissfully reassured that she was once again in step with the crowd. Dad told us excitedly that the Mini-Mart had almost completely sold out of Jelly Worms (though they still had plenty of Jelly Bears left), and that he was positive he had hit on something really big, something the Wall Street gurus hadn't noticed yet. He had the name of the manufacturer, the Kute Kandy Corporation of Wimberly, Pennsylvania, and he planned to call his broker first thing in the morning and buy stock in the company.

I will relieve the suspense by telling you that he bought a whole lot of Kute Kandy stock, and within a week, the price had doubled. Then it doubled again. Three weeks later, Dad sold his shares at four times the price he had paid for them. He made enough money to buy us a new car!

4

It was a book, *The Worm Turns*, that brought Beamer and me together. And it was another book that made us friends. Let me explain.

While Dad was busy watching the stock market, Beamer and I were observing the progression of the Jelly Worm fad. At lunch, we pretended we were anthropologists studying the curious customs of some exotic tribe. We got really scientific about it—counting how many kids had Jelly Worms each day and then plugging the numbers into a "Jelly Worm Fad Frequency Graph." It made a very pretty little sloping curve.

By late November, Jelly Worms were just a memory.

It was at about that time that Mrs. Lamb assigned our first book report. Now, generally speaking, kids my age tend to think that reading a book and then writing a one-page paper on it is about as much fun as washing a cat (I don't know why that is; it's my absolute favorite thing). So there was already a lot of negative feeling in the air. Mrs. Lamb added to it by saying that, since we were sixth graders now, she thought we were ready to stretch ourselves a bit.

Most of the time with book reports, you get to pick any book you want, though it usually has to be a certain number of pages, because otherwise, kids would do reports on *The Cat in the Hat* or something. But Mrs. Lamb wanted to make sure we all read something good. She handed out a list of twenty books for us to choose from.

More than half the class was already reading the latest book in the Chillers series, *Mind Wave*. Immediately, hands shot up all over the room. "Mrs. Lamb! Mrs. Lamb!" What everybody wanted to know was whether they could do the report on *Mind Wave* instead.

Mrs. Lamb wilted a little. Then she took a deep breath and said that while *Mind Wave* might be a fun book to read—and she herself was very fond of murder mysteries—still, we were stretching ourselves with this assignment. Remember?

Apparently, most of the kids in the class felt a certain lack of enthusiasm for stretching themselves, though they didn't say so out loud. There was a lot of slouching and grimacing. But Mrs. Lamb soldiered on.

The assignment had an added twist, she told us. We were to choose a partner, read the same book, then do the report together. The project would count as a major grade—the equivalent of two tests. Plus, there was opportunity for extra credit.

Now, since I already had a reputation as the girl who reads all the time, I was suddenly swamped with eager classmates who wanted to be my partner. This felt pretty good, I have to admit.

But I chose Beamer.

He suggested we read *Hatchet*—mostly, I suspect, because it was the shortest book on the list. I told him that I had already read *Hatchet*, though that wasn't the real reason I didn't want to choose it. See, I wanted the extra credit.

Most of the books on the list were on the sixth-grade reading level, some a bit harder. There were lots of Newbery winners and classics. But at the bottom of the page, there was one more book. If you chose that one and wrote a decent report on it, you got an extra twenty points added to your grade. So theoretically, you could make 120, which would do great things for your average, since the grade was counted twice.

And that wasn't all. As a reward for the extra time you were putting into the book report, you got an additional twenty points, which you could apply to your lowest test grade—in any subject!

Now, I figured I could use those extra points. Without going into any gory details, let me just say that math is not my thing. And twenty points is the difference between a *D* and a *B*. The only problem was how to convince Beamer to go along with my plan—because, you see, the book was *David Copperfield*.

"No way!" Beamer said.

I had expected that. I figured it might take some persuading. And, in fact, it took a lot of persuading. I think he only agreed to it in the end because he felt sorry for me, what with my math problem and all. That, and the fact that I volunteered to read the book aloud to him. "It'll be painless," I said.

"All right, Franny," he grumbled. "But you owe me."

After that, I went over to Beamer's house every afternoon to read *David Copperfield* to him.

Up until that time, I hadn't been to Beamer's house and he hadn't been to mine. We just hung out together at school. So I was kind of curious and excited to meet his parents and see what kind of house he lived in.

But before I met his parents *or* saw his house, I met Beamer's dogs. Five of them—I kid you not—in all sizes and breeds. Beamer said they all came from the ASPCA and would have been dead if his family hadn't adopted them.

The minute we opened the door, the dogs were waiting in the front hall, madly wagging their tails and barking and skipping around with excitement. The big dogs like to jump up and put their paws on your chest so they can lick you in the face and sniff you and drool on you. The smaller dogs dance around your feet, poking your ankles with their wet little noses. You have to be careful not to step on the little dogs while trying not to get knocked over by the big ones.

Once Beamer got the dogs calmed down, and we were safe to go into the house without stepping on someone's tail, I had a chance to look around.

Everything is really plain at Beamer's house. All the pictures and rugs and throw pillows and knickknacks my family packs up and moves from place to place—they didn't have any of those. He says his family likes it that way. They don't believe in having too many things— only what you really need. So the floors are bare wood and there aren't any curtains on the windows. Actually, after you get over the shock, it's really nice and sunny and restful there—or at least it would be if it weren't for the dogs.

As you might expect, there is a dog smell in the air, but that's sort of balanced out by the nice smell from the roses. That's the one thing (besides dogs) they have lots of—some in real vases and some in jelly jars. Beamer's mom owns a florist shop, called Perfect Petals, so they can have all the flowers they want.

Since Beamer's mom is busy at the shop all day, and since his dad is a drummer in a band and works at night, he's the one who is there in the afternoons.

Mr. Connolly is not your average dad. He has this really long hair, which makes him look like a hippie. He doesn't wear tie-dyed shirts or love beads or anything like that, but I bet he doesn't own a suit. I've never seen him in anything fancier than jeans and an old denim work shirt.

He does all the cooking for the family, and he's really good at it. He said he was thinking about going into catering someday, if the music business didn't pan out. I think he may have been showing off for me, just a little, but you should see what passes for after-school snacks at Beamer's house! Like, he baked these brownies, then cut them into shapes—stars and moons—and drizzled warm chocolate sauce over the plate in swirls. Then he dusted the whole thing with powdered sugar.

Every afternoon, after we'd eaten some fabulous snack, we'd go into Beamer's room. He has one of those kiddie gates set up in his doorway to keep the dogs out, because otherwise they'd mess with his stuff and drive him crazy. They're not all that easily discouraged, though. Maybe they think he'll change his mind some-day, so they just sit there, hanging their heads over the gate and staring at us—except for the littlest one, Cricket, who just peeks through the slats.

While I read *David Copperfield* to Beamer, he would work on his construction. A few years back, his parents bought him this building kit. It's got metal pieces—some are like bars and others are flat—with little nuts and bolts to hold them together. You're supposed to build bridges or skyscrapers with it, and each kit comes with all the stuff you need to make the Eiffel Tower or whatever is pictured on the box.

Well, Beamer decided he wanted to make his own thing, which doesn't look like anything you ever saw before. Beamer's dad calls it a "sculpture," which I guess is what it is. He's gone through four kits and is on the fifth, just adding shapes wherever he thinks it would look good. I'll tell you the truth: Beamer's sculpture looks better than a lot of stuff you see in museums. But it isn't finished yet. He says it's a "work in progress."

Beamer admitted that it was more fun to work on his construction with me reading to him—he said it kept two parts of his brain happy, whatever that means. He also admitted that he actually liked *David Copperfield*.

Granted, it's really long and some of the words are weird, since it was written a long time ago. But we got the hang of it pretty quickly, and from the first, we were never bored. In fact, Beamer and I got to where we hated to stop reading when my dad showed up to drive me home. We were dying to find out what would happen next—like my aunt Carol with her soap operas.

There are a lot of characters in *David Copperfield*. They usually have crazy names—like Traddles and Mr. Creakle—and every one of them is interesting in one way or another. Even the evil characters, and there are plenty of them. The story has lots of twists and turns and suspense and surprises and amazing coincidences. It's funny one minute and really sad the next. It just took my breath away.

All sorts of terrible things happen to poor David Copperfield, the main character. First, his father dies before he's even born; then his mother marries this horrible man, Mr. Murdstone, who beats David and sends him away. And then his mother dies and he is left penniless.

But he makes his way in the world with the help of his crazy aunt, Betsey Trotwood, who is always shooing donkeys away from her property, and Mr. Peggotty, who lives with his family in an upside-down boat, and Mr. Micawber, who has to hide from the bill collectors but is still very jolly and keeps expecting the money to "turn up" any day.

Then there are the villains—Mr. Murdstone, of course, and the awful Uriah Heep, who tells everybody how humble he is, only he's secretly planning to ruin kind Mr. Spenlow and steal all his money. David falls in love with *three* different girls, but he ends up with the right one just in time for a happy ending.

Now I know why Charles Dickens is such a famous author.

When the book was finally over, Beamer and I really missed it. It had made our lives more exciting for a while. All those dramatic things that happened to David—it was like they were happening to us, too, you see. Then the book ended and we were dropped back into our ordinary, boring lives.

Or so I thought.

There was a virus going around. Lots of kids went down to the nurse's office, rubbing their foreheads and groaning. They'd be out for a few days and then they'd be back, completely normal. Everybody who had had it said that there were no other symptoms. Just a really terrible headache that wouldn't go away, no matter what you took for it.

Zoë got it right at the start of the epidemic, and she was absolutely miserable. She lay in bed for days with the blinds down and a wet washcloth on her forehead. She said it felt like her head was about to explode.

I kept expecting to catch it, but I never did. Neither did my mom and dad. No one in Beamer's family was sick, either.

Later, when more than half the school was out with the headache, it was even reported on the news. Lots of other schools were experiencing the same thing. The news lady interviewed a doctor, who said there wasn't much you could do for it besides take Tylenol, get bed rest, and drink plenty of fluids.

Most of the kids had recovered and were back at school when I got the first hint of what was really going on. I had just come home from Beamer's and was heading down the hall to dump my backpack in my room. As I passed J.D.'s room, I saw him lying on the floor, with his feet up on the bed and his head resting on his favorite stuffed bear, holding a book in his hands.

I peeked my head in and asked what he was reading. He flipped the book around so I could see the cover. It was *Mind Wave*.

A couple of hours later, I heard J.D. let out this horrible moan. At first, I thought a lamp had fallen on him or something. But when I dashed into his room, I saw him sitting on the edge of his bed, clutching his head and groaning. He was even crying and—trust me on this—J.D. never cries.

"What?" I said.

"It feels like my head is going to explode," he moaned.

I called Mom and she hurried upstairs. Of course there wasn't much she could do to help him, but she did give him some Tylenol and a wet cloth to put on his forehead. Then she tucked him into bed and turned out the lights. She put her finger to her lips, indicating I should be really quiet and let him rest.

I went back to my room and lay down to think. There was something tickling my mind, something important I knew I would figure out if I just kept very quiet and concentrated. It was what J.D. had said—that he felt like his head was about to explode. Zoë had said it, too, in almost the exact same words. Now, I know people exaggerate when they feel bad; they say they think they're going to die and stuff like that. But I had the feeling that this was different. And it reminded me of something I had heard kids talking about at school. I hadn't paid all that much attention—still . . . exploding heads . . .

After a while, I couldn't stand it anymore. I tiptoed into J.D.'s room and patted his arm.

"How're you doing?" I whispered.

"Horrible," he said.

"J.D.," I said, "can I just ask you one question? And then I promise I'll leave you alone."

He just sort of grunted. I took that for a yes.

"That book you were reading, did it have anything

in it about an exploding head?"

Big sigh. Then, reluctantly, "Yes."

Wow!

"Thanks, J.D.," I said. "Try to go to sleep, if you can." I crept out of the room and closed the door very quietly. Then I ran downstairs and picked up the phone.

"Beamer!" I said. "You want to hear this really, really weird idea I just had?"

"Go for it," he said.

"Well, you know that book *Mind Wave*? The new I. M. Fine book?"

"Yes."

"Well, it's about an exploding head."

"Thanks for sharing that."

"No, wait. I haven't gotten to the weird part yet. J.D. was reading it this afternoon, and tonight he came down with that horrible headache that's been going around. Beamer, I think that's what's causing the head-aches!"

"What, the book?"

"Yes."

"You're right—that is totally weird."

"Come on, Beamer, think about it. The last I. M. Fine book caused the Jelly Worm fad."

"Yeah, but that's totally different," he said. "Kids

thought it was fun to play with Jelly Worms because they were in that book and they ate Cleveland or whatever. Like it was really hilarious. But nobody's going to read a story about an exploding head and say, 'Way, cool! I think I'll have a headache!'"

"Yeah, I know it isn't logical. But I just have this *feeling.*"

"Yeah, well," Beamer said. Then there was this long pause.

"All right," I said. "Forget I even mentioned it."

I couldn't get to sleep that night, thinking about *Mind Wave* and the headaches. I had to admit that Beamer was probably right—my idea was way out there in cuckooland. And yet . . . I just couldn't let it go. Finally, I decided it wouldn't hurt to gather a little information.

So the next day, I started casually asking some of the kids who had been sick—Jacob and Mark and Felicia and lots more—if they had read the book. Every one of them said yes. I wrote it all down in my notebook. Then I started asking other kids, every chance I got—like on the playground or in the lunchroom—whether they had gotten the terrible headache and whether they had read the book. By the end of the day, I had it all down in writing. Out of the twenty-three people I had asked, there was a perfect correlation. Everyone who had read the book had gotten the headache. Nobody who hadn't read the book had gotten the headache. You have to admit, those are pretty impressive numbers!

That afternoon, at Beamer's house, I pulled out my notebook and showed it to him.

"Come on, Beamer," I said. "Check this out—one hundred percent!"

He raised his eyebrows and kind of shrugged. "It's interesting," he said, "but, Franny, it doesn't make any sense at all. How could you get a headache from reading a book?"

"I don't know," I said. "Maybe it works by suggestion. Like when someone yawns, you have to yawn, too. Sometimes all you have to do is say the word *yawn* to make it happen."

This made us both yawn and laugh, more or less at the same time.

"Right, but a yawn is one thing. A splitting headache that lasts for three days is something else."

"True," I admitted. "But will you admit that the numbers are really amazing?"

"Yes."

"But you don't like my explanation?"

"Not really."

35

"Maybe the description of the head explosion is really, really vivid."

"Maybe you should read it and find out," he said.

So I did.

And at first, I remembered exactly why I had liked the Chillers books so much. The story was really exciting. And though it wasn't *David Copperfield* or anything, I couldn't put it down.

Basically, here's the plot: There is this family, and they are all happy because they have just bought a new microwave oven. Only what they don't realize is that this is no ordinary microwave oven. It sends out these bizarre pulsing waves that make everybody in the house get headaches. The worst headaches happen when people are thinking bad thoughts.

Then one night, the parents go out and the kids are left alone with this really demonic baby-sitter. She makes the kids go to their rooms, even though they haven't done anything wrong. She just doesn't want them to bother her while she's watching TV and talking to her boyfriend on the phone. She decides to raid the cupboard for something to eat, and she finds some microwave popcorn. So she's standing there, watching through the little window and listening to the popping, when all of a sudden she grabs her head with both hands and screams. The kids run down the stairs and into the kitchen just in time to see her *head explode!*

That was as far as I got. My head started throbbing. It hurt like crazy. I tried taking deep breaths, and lying down with a pillow over my eyes. But it just got worse and worse, until I started moaning and wailing and my parents came in to see what was going on.

They did all they could for me, just like they had for Zoë and J.D. They tried Tylenol, ice packs, soft music, complete silence, back rubs, orange juice—the whole nine yards. Let me tell you, nothing worked. I wanted to call Beamer and say, "See!" only I was too miserable to move.

After three days of moaning and weeping and three nights of fitful sleep, I awoke one morning and felt absolutely, positively normal.

Mom made me stay home one more day, since I was really tired from not getting enough sleep. And it's kind of fun, staying home from school when you feel perfectly fine. I watched a lot of television and napped some. At about four o'clock, I called Beamer.

"Thanks for the suggestion," I said.

"I called you—only your mom said you were too sick to come to the phone."

"That's the understatement of the century!"

"Are you okay now?"

"Yeah, magically, I am okay. But I have a book you might want to read. Just to see what happens."

"Franny . . ."

"What?"

"It doesn't prove anything. Except that you read that book expecting something bad to happen, and it did."

"You know what, Beamer? In the immortal words of Bart Simpson, 'Eat my shorts!'" Then I hung up. It was a really stupid thing to say, but it made me feel brilliant for about half an hour.

6

Since Beamer didn't believe me, I decided to try my dad. After all, he was the one who was so impressed by I. M. Fine's powers of persuasion.

That night over dinner, I laid the whole thing out step by step, beginning with the connection between the Jelly Worm fad and *The Worm Turns*. Then I moved on to the amazing numerical correlation between readers of *Mind Wave* and the horrible headaches. I finished up with a description of my own personal experience, to which J.D. and Zoë added gory details of their own. The more I talked, the more I was sure they would have to believe me.

"Honey," my mom said, "I really don't think this has anything to do with those books. It was just a virus."

"A virus that only struck children who were reading this one book? A book about an exploding head?"

Now my dad chimed in. "Franny, let's say I slip and fall on the stairs just as you turn on the radio—do you assume the radio caused my fall?"

I rolled my eyes. "No . . ." I said. "Unless the radio was really, really loud and I blasted you with it all of a sudden and scared you so that you lost your balance."

"That's how superstitions get started," Dad said. "Like this one: It's winter and it's cold outside. People get sick. They decide that cold weather causes colds. Hence the name."

"Well, doesn't it?" asked Zoë.

"No, viruses cause colds. They even did a study where people stood barefoot in draughty hallways, went outside in the winter with wet hair, all those things that old wives say will make you 'catch your death.' It didn't do anything. It's just that people congregate more inside during the winter and pass germs back and forth."

"Whatever," I said.

"Don't say 'whatever,' Franny. I'm just trying to help you think scientifically."

"That's all right," I said, discouraged. "Never mind."

The next day, I was back at school. Nobody made a big fuss over me, since practically the whole class had been home with the same thing and it was already old news. I was a little embarrassed to face Beamer after the "Eat my shorts" remark, so at lunch, I went out on the playground and ate by myself. It would pass, I knew, because Beamer and I had the kind of friendship that doesn't fall apart over little things. I just needed to get my dignity back and work a few things out in my head, that was all.

Like, for instance, what was going on with the I. M. Fine books? Unfortunately, it was clear I would have to figure it out by myself.

After school, I did not go to Beamer's house. Instead, I hopped on my bike and went to the library. I thought—what the heck!—I would look up I. M. Fine in *Something About the Author*. Who knew what I might find?

Well, nothing, as it turned out. I. M. Fine wasn't even listed—and this was a guy who had published thirty-six books!

I went over to the shelf where all his books were kept and picked one up. I have to admit that I did it with a certain dread—like I thought it would bite me or something. Of course nothing happened. It was just a regular paperback, though pretty ragged from being handled by so many readers. I checked the back cover, but there was nothing there about I. M. Fine. Just stuff about the other titles in the series.

Sometimes, with paperbacks, they put the author's bio on the last page, so I looked there, too. Nothing.

The librarian came up behind me and looked over my shoulder. "So, are you a fan of I. M. Fine?"

"No!" I practically shrieked. Well, see, she kind of startled me.

The librarian smiled. She didn't ask why, if that was the case, I was standing there holding a copy of *Meet My Mummy*, number twenty-seven, by I. M. Fine.

"I'm just trying to figure something out," I explained. "I mean, here's this guy who's so famous and has written all these books—and he's not in *Something About the Author*."

"Really? That *is* odd," the librarian admitted.

"Can you think of any reason why he wouldn't be?"

"Well," she said. "I wonder. You know, sometimes books in a series are actually written by a whole flock of different writers. The publisher gives them a plot outline to follow. I know they did that with the Nancy Drew books. There never really was an author named Carolyn Keene. It was just a name they made up."

"Wow," I said. "Maybe that's it—maybe there is no I. M. Fine. That would explain why he's not listed."

"Yes," the librarian agreed. "It would."

I thanked the librarian and went home, feeling strangely unsatisfied.

You see, while her theory explained why I. M. Fine wasn't listed in *Something About the Author,* and it also explained how he could write them so fast, it didn't explain all the other stuff. For example, if you just had a bunch of writers cranking out stories according to some formula, then any strange effects the books were having on their readers had to be an accident. And that seemed unlikely, somehow. I mean, why didn't other books have the same effects? What was so special about Chillers?

On the other hand, the accident theory was comforting. I mean, it would be better than if there really was some psycho guy out there making weird things happen on purpose! And since I liked that theory better and had pretty much hit a dead end anyway, I decided to forget the whole stupid thing and get on with my life.

And I did, too, for a while—until the business with the snakes.

In March, book number thirty-seven in the Chillers
series was published. It was called *Sinister Serpent
Surprise.*

The weather was unusually warm, though naturally
the school thermostat was still set for winter, so hot air
was being pumped in through the vents at full throttle,
till we thought we'd all suffocate. Mrs. Lamb had to
open all the windows just so we could breathe. I looked
at Beamer several times, back there in the last row,
slumped down in his seat, with those long legs sprawling
out into the aisle. He was gazing out the window, like he
was a million miles away. Probably creating construc-
tions in his head. If I'd been close enough, I would have
poked him. I wasn't, though, so I didn't.

The morning dragged on miserably. I think the only thing that kept us going was the prospect of lunch. Beamer and I ate out on the far side of the playground, where there are a few trees and a nice cool grassy place to sit. There was even a little breeze.

Then the bell rang and we trudged back to the classroom.

During the lunch break, Mrs. Lamb had put some math problems up on the board. I guess she figured that going up there to solve them was more entertaining than sitting at our desks doing work sheets.

She asked Adam, Claire, and DeeDee to go first. They all went up to the board, got some chalk, and went to work. I secretly enjoyed watching DeeDee do this, because for once she was the one on the spot. I'm no great shakes at math, but compared to DeeDee, I'm a regular Einstein. She went through all sorts of poses as she studied the problem (resting chin in hand, crossing arms and leaning back for a really good look, tapping her teeth), but she didn't come up with an answer.

Adam and Claire finished their problems and went back to their seats. DeeDee just stood there, chalk in gracefully upraised hand, smiling beautifully, with her eyebrows raised in a positively adorable plea for help. This never failed. Mrs. Lamb went over and talked her through the problem.

"Okay, DeeDee," she said, "nine times five is . . ."

"Forty . . . forty-five?"

"That's right."

DeeDee beamed.

"So put down the five and carry the four." Mrs. Lamb showed DeeDee where to put the four.

"Now, nine times eight is . . ."

"Ssss . . ." DeeDee said.

"Seventy . . ."

"Sssssssssssssssss!" DeeDee said, only now she had dropped the chalk and was beginning to slide down toward the floor. Mrs. Lamb just stood there, stunned, while everybody gasped.

"SSSSSSSSSSSSSSSSSSSS!" DeeDee hissed, and she was stretched out on the linoleum now, slithering like a snake. Her skirt rode up, so you could see her panties; her beautiful hair was dragging around in the chalk dust under the board.

Mrs. Lamb knelt down and took DeeDee's face in her hands to keep it from thrashing around. "Will somebody please run get the nurse," she said urgently. "I think she might be having a seizure."

"I'll go," I said, and leapt out of my seat. But before I could reach the door, Jonah rolled out onto the floor

46

and began hissing and slithering, too.

"NOW!" shouted Mrs. Lamb. "Hurry!"

I practically killed myself tripping over backpacks and Beamer's legs on the way to the door. Once I was out in the hall, I heard the sound of hissing coming from other rooms. I took off in a dash down the hall. To my left, a door opened and out came a third grader with a panicked expression on his little round face. We sprinted side by side the rest of the way to the nurse's office.

I knew, even before I opened the door, what I would find in there. I could hear it. But I had been sent to fetch the nurse, and my brain was slow to adjust to a new plan. The infirmary was like the snake pit at the zoo. The floor was filled with writhing, slithering students. The nurse gave me a frantic look and shut the door. "I'm busy!" she said.

Well, obviously.

I put my hand to my chest and took a big, deep breath. Then I headed for the principal's office, with the third grader trailing behind me in tears. I knocked.

"Not now!" called a voice from inside. I opened the door anyway. Mrs. Jessup was holding the telephone receiver with one hand and a pale, writhing, hissing child with the other.

"Hang up and dial 911," I said.

She didn't have a free hand to wave me away, so she sort of bared her fangs at me.

"Yes, please get here as soon as you can!" she was saying into the phone. "You will probably need to take her to the emergency room. . . . No, I have no idea. Really. Please just get here as soon as you can!" Then she hung up and got a better grip on the little girl, who was hissing loudly and sliding back down toward the floor.

"Can't you see I'm busy!" she shouted.

"Dial 911!" I repeated. "She's not the only one. The infirmary is full of them. This is going on *all over the school*!" She looked at me for a moment in stunned disbelief, then dialed the emergency number.

"This is Martha Jessup at Park Place Intermediate. We have something strange going on here. . . . A large number of students seem to be having seizures or something."

After a pause, she said, "No, it's more like—well, this will sound really strange, but it's as if they're pretending to be snakes. Slithering, hissing."

I was sure the emergency personnel on the other end of the line could hear the hissing perfectly well. It was very loud.

"Oh, no. I hadn't considered that. It has been very

hot in the building, but I don't smell any fumes or anything. And I believe that most of the kids are fine. Should we take them all outside till the ambulances come?"

Another pause.

"I couldn't begin to tell you," she said. Then she looked up at me. "How many, do you think?"

"Well, two in my class. . . ." I turned to the third grader, who was cowering in terror behind me. "How many in yours?"

"Just Alicia," he whimpered.

"That's three, plus this one." I indicated the child in the principal's arms. "At least seven in the infirmary, and I heard hissing all down the hall. I'd guess at least fifteen, but maybe a whole lot more."

"Did you hear that?" Mrs. Jessup said into the phone. "Send as many as you can."

She hung up and flipped on the loudspeaker. "May I have your attention!" she said. "We are having a medical emergency here. Teachers, will you please assist your affected students out onto the front lawn. The rest of you, please stay with your teacher and exit the building in an orderly manner. I repeat: Walk, don't run, but please leave the building."

It was a madhouse, of course. The principal and I

managed to get the little girl outside; then Mrs. Jessup went back in to help get more kids out. I was impressed by how fast the ambulances came. Hissing students were fitted with neck braces and loaded onto stretchers, two or three per ambulance. A few of the kids who had been just fine when they left the building suddenly fell down and started hissing, too.

While they waited in little clusters outside the school, a couple of the teachers started passing their cell phones around so the students could call their parents. Within minutes, frantic moms arrived in droves, managing to block the exit, so the ambulances couldn't get out. Mr. Clark, the PE teacher, had to wade into the mess and direct traffic.

I stood there in the midst of all that bedlam, wondering what to do. I couldn't find Zoë or J.D. Beamer offered to give me a ride home, but who knew when his dad would arrive? I was on the verge of freaking out.

"Thanks, Beamer," I said, "but I need to get out of here now."

So I walked home.

I was sitting at the kitchen table, eating a bowl of cereal, when it hit me. You're probably way ahead of me here, but please understand, it had been a pretty traumatic experience.

It was I. M. Fine again.

I thought about it and thought about it—and I couldn't stand not having somebody to tell. Finally, the phone rang. It was Beamer.

"I bet I know what you're thinking" was the first thing he said.

"Yeah, I bet you do," I answered.

"*Sinister Serpent Surprise.* Kind of a coincidence, huh?"

"Do you believe me now?"

There was a long pause on the other end. "Well," he said, "let's just agree that it is an amazing coincidence. Worth looking into."

"Thanks for that vote of confidence, Beamer."

"What about Zoë and J.D.?" he asked. "Are they okay?"

"I don't know," I said, "Nobody's home. And I can't reach Mom on her cell phone, either. I bet she's gone over to school to pick us up."

Just then, I heard a little beep. Call waiting.

"Maybe that's her," I said. "Let me call you back." I clicked over to the other line.

"Franny, are you all right?" It was Mom.

"I'm fine," I said. "It was pretty awful over at the school, so I walked home. I hope I didn't scare you."

"That's all right. Your teacher told me you left. I just wanted to make sure you got home safely."

"Did you find Zoë and J.D.?"

"Yes," she said. "They're here with me. But, Franny, we're over at the hospital. Zoë had some kind of strange episode. . . ."

"Zoë!" I practically screamed.

"Franny, calm down. Quite a few kids are here with the same thing. Well, you were there. You saw what was going on."

"The hissing and slithering . . ."

"Yes. They thought it might be some kind of seizure, but her EEG is perfectly normal. They may run a few more tests, but the doctor seems to feel it's not serious."

"Okay," I said numbly.

"I need to hang up now and call Dad. I'd like him to come get J.D. and take him home. There's no telling how long this will take. And don't worry. Zoë is going to be fine. I'll keep you posted."

She hung up. I finished my cereal, then went into the living room and turned on the TV, switching channels for something to do.

Dad and J.D. came home after a while and joined me in front of the TV.

Mom called again to say that Zoë was much better. She was a little groggy, but she was resting peacefully. They would be home in an hour or two. She suggested that maybe we should order in some pizza.

So we were sitting there, flipping channels, when suddenly I froze. There was a news lady, reporting live, with a crowd of kids in the background. Several of them were lying in the grass, hissing and slithering like snakes.

"That's our school!" J.D. yelled.

The camera panned in for a close-up.

"Ambulances are being diverted to outlying hospitals,"

the reporter was saying, "due to the massive number of cases that are coming in."

"Look!" J.D. said. He had seen it at the same moment I had. There were letters on the side of the brick building. They said WILL ROGERS MIDDLE SCHOOL.

"It's not our school!" I said. "This is happening other places!"

The phone rang. It was Beamer.

"Turn on the news!" I said.

"I did," he replied breathlessly. "It's on CNN, too."

"You're kidding. It's not just in Baltimore?"

"No, Franny, it's *all over the country!*"

I gasped. I said a bad word.

"Beamer—"

"Yes."

"Zoë's in the hospital."

"With the snake thing?"

"Yeah. But Mom keeps saying she's fine. It's really creepy, though."

"Gosh, I'm sorry, Franny." I could hear voices in the background. "Wait a minute—hold on. My dad's yelling something." There was a pause. "Turn on NBC."

"Okay," I said, and hung up.

There was a man in a white coat standing behind a

podium, talking to reporters. Letters at the bottom of the screen identified him as a professor of neurology at the Johns Hopkins School of Medicine.

"No," he was saying, "we feel certain that there is nothing here that points to terrorism. At the moment, we are treating it as some sort of mass psychogenic episode, though, to be honest, we have never seen anything quite like this before, so we are just trying to stay calm and not jump to any conclusions."

There was a hubbub of voices, lots of reporters asking questions at the same time. The doctor nodded his head slightly, indicating that he had heard at least one question that he could decipher, and then started talking again.

"Well," he said, "the symptoms are quite genuine; let me emphasize that. But the trigger could have been emotional rather than physical. Which is what we mean by 'psychogenic.' There have certainly been cases of this before, one as recently as 1998, when a large number of children fell ill at a school after someone thought he smelled fumes. However, no physical agent was ever found.

"The good news is that the children we have seen here have recovered on their own, with no perceptible ill effects. Nevertheless, the widespread nature of the outbreak and the degree to which it has been limited almost entirely to elementary and middle school children suggest that we need to explore the matter further. The Centers for Disease Control and Prevention will undoubtedly be looking into it."

The reporters shouted questions again, the word *snake* clearly audible from several.

"It has been mentioned that the behavior of the children was snakelike, by which I mean falling to the floor and moving in a slithering sort of motion, combined with emitting a hissing sound. This could also be explained by mass hysteria—if I may use that term. And I would like to point out that such behavior is nothing new, historically speaking. Three hundred years ago, in Salem, Massachusetts, there were instances of perfectly normal children getting on all fours and barking like dogs. Their sincere belief that they were being possessed by demons took any number of bizarre forms. Fear can have a profound effect on vulnerable individuals such as children."

He went on like that for a few more minutes. There wasn't really anything new to say, and soon the reporters started bringing up the usual crackpot theories—like maybe Iraq had sprayed America with Ebola virus, or the kids had been poisoned by genetically altered food—all of which the doctor denied. He began to look exasperated and brought the press conference to a close. The station switched back to the footage taken at Will Rogers Middle School earlier in the day and repeated the basic story for those who had just tuned in.

"Call me when the pizza arrives," I told Dad, and headed upstairs to think.

Things had definitely changed.

For starters, I was now absolutely, positively sure there was a direct connection between the Chillers books and the strange stuff that was going on. Three books in a row, and all of them having some unusual widespread effect on the kids who read them. . . . A coincidence? Uh-uh.

What was even scarier, no accidental effect could be that consistent. This was being done on purpose. And that being the case, it followed that we were talking about a real, actual person, not a committee of ghostwriters—well, not unless that committee was part of a conspiracy, and even I wasn't ready to be that paranoid.

The other thing I couldn't help noticing was that these weird events were escalating. In a pretty short time, we'd gone from a harmless candy fad to ambulances rushing kids to hospitals, my own sister included. What would happen when the next book came out?

All of this left me pondering the big question: What could I do about it?

See, the whole business sounds so off-the-wall when you actually put it into words—like something out of the *X-Files*. So it wasn't all that likely that the police or the president or anybody like that would believe me. I mean, my own parents hadn't. Even Beamer hadn't believed me at first. J.D. was the only one who'd really swallowed my theory outright, and he was only ten.

So it looked like anything that got done would get done by us: me and Beamer and J.D. Not exactly the FBI! But you work with what you've got. And somehow, we had to find I. M. Fine and convince him to stop.

We began by writing him a letter in care of his publisher. Just a regular fan letter—to smoke him out. Then, while we waited for the reply, we got on the Internet.

On his publisher's website, we found a complete list of his books, but no biographical information. We looked for him on the list of authors with personal websites and in the section on how to get an author to visit your school. I'm sure you've already guessed—he wasn't in either of those places.

Next, we tried to track him down through several "find a person" sites on the web. We were glad his name wasn't Robert Smith or Michael Johnson. After all, how many people could there be named I. M. Fine?

Well, none, as it turned out. We did find quite a few people named Fine with first names that began with the letter *I*. There were lots of Irvings, several Irvins, plus a sprinkling of Ivys and Isaacs and Irises and Irenes. There was an Isidore, an Inca, and an Ilona. Several were just listed as I. Fine, and a few with two initials: I.D., I.F., and I.B.—but no I.M. They lived all over—from Pompano Beach, Florida, to Van Nuys, California, and everywhere in between.

If we had wanted to—and if we'd had a credit card and $39.95 to spend—we could have found out all kinds of things about these people: every one of their previous addresses for the past ten years, their physical descriptions as listed on their driver's licenses, the names of their family members, the names and phone numbers of their neighbors, what property they owned (and how much it was worth), what kind of car they drove (and how much it was worth), and whether they had ever been sued in court or had filed for bankruptcy.

All of which I find extremely creepy, if you want to know the truth. We looked up my dad's name, just out of curiosity—and there he was, along with our home address. So anybody with $39.95 who wanted to play private eye could delve into our private lives. They could find out my mom's name and my name, and Zoë's and J.D.'s, too. They could find out what color my dad's hair and eyes are, how tall he is, and that he has to wear glasses to drive. They could even phone our neighbors and ask questions about us. It's like something out of a spy story, only it's real. Some weirdo could look you up, too. Think about it.

Okay, I realize that I'm in no position to complain about people snooping on other people, since that was exactly what we were doing. But I think you will agree that we were doing it for a very good reason.

"Surely you're not planning to contact every one of those people and ask them if they wrote the Chillers books?" Beamer said.

It did seem pretty pointless. After all, if he wasn't listed in *Something About the Author* and didn't have his bio on his books, then he was probably trying to protect himself from his fans—truckloads of mail, kids ringing his doorbell, that sort of thing.

"Beamer!" I said. "I can't believe I didn't think of this before. You know where they get all those names, don't you? From phone books all over the country. I. M. Fine isn't going to have his number listed. Famous people never do."

"Yeah, you're right," Beamer agreed. "We sure wasted a lot of time."

About a week later, the letter from the publisher came. It was a form letter, very cheery and pleasant, basically saying that I. M. Fine was a shy person and didn't wish to be in the spotlight, and that he was too busy writing those wonderful books to make public appearances or to write to children. At the author's specific request, no biographical material was ever released. However, information on all the past books in the series was enclosed, along with exciting information about the *next* book, to be published in June. It was going to be called *The Ghost of Creepy Hollow.*

"Where's Creepy Hollow?" asked J.D.

"It's a joke," I explained. "You know—like 'The Legend of Sleepy Hollow.'"

"Where's Sleepy Hollow?"

"I don't know, J.D.—nowhere. The author made it up."

"Oh," he said, disappointed.

"All right, guys. Let's focus. What have we accomplished?"

"Nothing," said J.D.

We all sat there looking glum. We needed a new plan, and nobody had one.

After about ten minutes, during which we all stared into space, Beamer made a suggestion.

"How about the library? There must be books besides *Something About the Author* that have stuff on famous people Maybe he's listed in one of them."

"Yeah," I said. "It's worth a try. *Who's Who* and like that."

So, since that was our one and only idea, we headed for the library.

When we got there, I showed J.D. the section where all the I. M. Fine books were kept. I told him it was his job to go through the books in a systematic manner and check the backs for biographical material. I figured that would keep him out of trouble while we were in the reference section. Then we went to find the nice librarian I had talked to before.

"Hi," I said. "Remember me?"

"Yes, of course," she said. "Still interested in I. M. Fine?"

I nodded. "That's why we're here, actually. Some

stuff has happened, and it turns out we were wrong about that committee of ghostwriters. I. M. Fine is definitely real."

"Oh?" she said. "What kind of 'stuff'?"

"Well, you remember when everybody got that snake sickness? It was on the news and all?"

"The seizures? Yes, I remember."

"Well, do you also remember the name of the I. M. Fine book that came out at the very same time?"

"No . . ." she said slowly. "I don't actually."

"*Sinister Serpent Surprise!*" I said, knowing even as I spoke that she was not going to say "Wow!"

"Really. . . ." She was trying not to smile. "And you think there's a connection?"

"Never mind," I said. "We just want to look him up in some of your reference books—besides *Something About the Author.* What else have you got?"

"Come on," she said, and led us to the reference section. "I'll show you." She pulled out a book called *Major Authors and Illustrators for Children and Young Adults* and another one called *Who's Who Among North American Authors.* "That's all I have," she said, "but there will be others at the central branch."

We thanked her and settled down at one of the big library tables.

"It's probably best if you don't try to explain it to people, Franny. They're just going to think we're nuts."

"I know," I said defensively. "It just sort of slipped out."

Beamer shoved *Who's Who* over to my side of the table and leaned back in his chair. "You're the designated reader," he said.

For better or for worse, I realized, this wasn't going to take all that long. I mean, there were only two books. And if we came up empty, we were clean out of ideas.

I opened *Who's Who* and turned to the *F* section. I double-checked just to be sure, then heaved a big sigh.

"Not there?"

"Nope. Man, this guy is really, *really* determined to be mysterious."

"This is true," Beamer agreed.

"Hand me *Major Authors* and let's get this over with." I didn't have very high hopes. Still, I had to go through the motions.

I thumbed through the pages. Farley . . . Feelings . . . Feiffer . . . FINE!

I couldn't believe it. Fine, I. M.—right there in black and white!

The thrill lasted about two seconds. Under his name, where I should have found his date and place of birth, name of spouse and children, educational institutions attended, and all that other interesting stuff, was a single statement: "Personal information withheld at the author's request." There followed a list of his published works, and that was it.

"Well, great!" I said, slamming the book closed and causing several people to turn and stare. "Just great!"

Beamer had slid so far down in his chair, I thought he might disappear under the table. "Maybe we should forget this and do something else," he said. "Start a rock band. Take up racquetball."

I got up and put the books back on the shelf.

"Let's get J.D. and go home," I said. "This is too depressing."

We found him exactly where we'd left him. He was sitting on the floor, surrounded by a pile of ratty paperbacks with lurid covers. He was gazing at one particularly hideous illustration of a disembodied mouth the size of a van, with a huge tongue protruding from it. Spit was oozing out onto the sidewalk, where several terrified children were reacting more or less as you might expect. He looked up as we came over and grinned.

"Hey, check this out!" he said.

"J.D., that's gross."

He shrugged and put the book down.

"We're getting out of here," I said. "Come on, we'll help you clean this mess up." Beamer and I got down on the rug and started gathering up the books and putting them away on the shelf.

Suddenly, J.D. turned to me with a big grin and said, "Oh! Guess what!"

"What?"

"*Wim*-ber-ly, Penn-syl-*van*-ia!" He rolled the words off his tongue like he was playing Shakespeare.

"Say again?"

"Wimberly, Pennsylvania," he repeated. "That's where he lives."

I picked up the mouth book and looked at the back. There was nothing there but the usual ad for other books in the series. "Where?" I snapped.

"Not that one," he said, taking it out of my hand. "This one."

The book he handed me looked different from the others. It didn't say Chillers on the cover, for one thing, though it was clearly a horror story. The picture showed two anxious-looking boys cowering in front of a crumbling Victorian mansion. *Ghost Walk*, it was called. I flipped it over. There were two paragraphs on the back telling the plot of the book and trying to make you want to buy it.

"Look at the last page," J.D. said. So I did.

"I. M. Fine lives in Wimberly, Pennsylvania," it said.

Wow! It must have been his very first book. Before Chillers even started. Before he became famous. Before he went underground.

"Great work, J.D.," I said. "Our first real break! Now we have something to go on." Then I stopped gushing for a minute, because something was tickling my memory.

"Say—guys! Doesn't that name ring a bell with you? Wimberly, Pennsylvania?"

"Not with me," said J.D.

"Well, I've heard of it," Beamer said. "It's near where my grandparents live. Pretty small. Kind of on the outskirts of Philadelphia."

"Yeah, but that's not it. It's familiar to me, too—and I never met your grandparents."

I sat down on the floor beside J.D., amid the scattered books, closed my eyes, and thought. Where had I heard that name before?

Then it came to me. Kute Kandy Corporation. Jelly Worms.

"Guys," I said, "you're not going to believe this!"

10

About a week after school let out, Beamer's mom and dad drove us up to Harper's Mill, Pennsylvania. That's where his grandparents live. Beamer goes there every summer to visit for a couple of weeks. This time, he asked if he could bring a friend.

Now, as much as I enjoy spending time with Beamer, I wouldn't normally go hinting around for an invitation to join him on a trip to visit his grandparents, which is exactly what I did. But I had my reasons.

You see, Beamer spends his days at the community swimming pool when he's there, since his grandmother still works and his grandfather is busy with this invention business he has out in the garage. The swimming pool is nice, Beamer said, with a snack bar and all. And he knows some of the town kids, and they're nice, too.

All of which was beside the point, as far as I was concerned. The key thing to know about the Harper's Mill swimming pool—and the reason I wanted to go there—is that it's a short walk to the bus station. And by bus, it's less than a half-hour ride to Wimberly, Pennsylvania—home of I. M. Fine.

Now, I was fully aware that Beamer's grandparents probably wouldn't approve of the two of us running off to Wimberly to stalk a famous author—though they wouldn't have to know about it, of course. And for that matter, I hadn't exactly gotten Beamer to agree to it, either. But I would. I was sure of it.

So there we were, barreling along the highway, listening to moldy oldies on the radio, when suddenly something flashed through my mind. Something I had forgotten to consider, what with planning to hunt down I. M. Fine and all. It was this: I was about to spend two whole weeks with a pair of complete strangers. And, Beamer or no Beamer, I was going to feel like the duck at the dog's picnic.

To make things worse, these weren't merely complete strangers; they were elderly complete strangers. The house, I suddenly knew, would be dark and smell of cats. Every surface would be covered with little china knickknacks. The grandmother would hover over me constantly, afraid I would stain the sofa or drop crumbs on her carpet. The food would be soft and bland. At night, we would watch reruns of *I Love Lucy*.

I should have known better.

No cats, it turned out, no knickknacks, no clutter. Just this very modern house, with ceilings so high and walls so stark and plain that you felt like you were in a church or a museum. Every room had sliding glass doors that looked out onto the woods, making you feel like you were in a tree house.

The Gordons were more than just kind to me. From the way they acted, you'd think that I was a movie star or maybe a princess, and that I was doing them this great favor by inviting myself to spend two weeks at their house. I felt really bad remembering all the negative thoughts I'd had on the drive up there.

That night, we had Chinese takeout Mrs. Gordon had brought in from Philadelphia on her way home from work. This was the usual way of things at their house. On the weekends, Mrs. Gordon cooked. Every other night, the food came from restaurants. None of it was regular American food, either. You name it, we ate it: Indian food, Chinese, Mexican, Italian—even this Japanese stuff called sushi, which has raw fish in it.

Mrs. Gordon took the food out of the Styrofoam containers and served it in pretty bowls. We ate at the table with linen place mats and silver and candles and everything. It was like being at a party.

At about 9:30, Beamer's grandparents said good night. They belonged to the "early to bed, early to rise" school of thought. Mrs. Gordon threw us a kiss as she headed down the hall.

"Wow, Beamer, your grandparents are so sweet!" I said.

"Yeah," he agreed. "It's genetic. That's where I got all my sweetness."

I punched his arm—in a friendly sort of way, you understand.

He reached for the remote control and turned on the TV.

"Beamer," I said cautiously.

"What?"

"Um . . . tomorrow."

"'Um . . . tomorrow,' what?"

"Well, I was thinking. I mean, part of the reason I'm here is . . . well, shouldn't we be planning a trip to Wimberly?"

He sighed and made a little face.

"I don't know, Franny," he said. "The thought of

taking a bus to Wimberly and bothering some writer guy feels kind of creepy to me."

"Not as creepy as what might happen if we don't."

"Yeah, maybe," he said.

"Come on, Beamer. It won't be creepy. It'll be fun. We'll get to meet a famous author!"

"And make him hate us."

"Well, I bet you've never been hated by a famous author before."

Beamer gave me *the look*.

"You thought it was a good idea two months ago."

"Yeah—only now it feels really creepy. And what I really want to do tomorrow is go to the pool—okay? And right now, I want to watch TV."

He grabbed the remote and started flipping channels. We both sat there watching as one image flowed into another. Somebody giving a speech. Somebody selling gold earrings. A rerun of *E. R.* A talking head. Another talking head. A car commercial. A sitcom of some young people sitting around in a living room. Somebody praying. A lipstick commercial. An animal documentary.

I just kept my mouth shut. Why spoil the moment?

11

We got to the pool early, before the heat of the day had set in and the crowds had arrived to take all the lounge chairs. We slathered on sunblock, dragged two chairs into the shade of a big leafy tree, and got comfortable. I closed my eyes and listened to the peaceful sounds of summer—water splashing, the occasional squeal of a baby, and the swish of the wind in the trees. I promptly fell asleep.

At around eleven o'clock, lots of kids started arriving and the snack bar opened. We bought hamburgers and fries and sodas and candy bars and took them over to our chairs to eat. A couple of kids came over and said hi to Beamer and he introduced us.

One of them was a girl named Allison. She had

black hair and freckles and looked like she worked out at a gym or something. You know, strong.

"Are you still diving?" Beamer asked.

"Yeah," she said. "And swimming."

"She can't get into her room, for all the trophies," another girl said.

"Oh, shut up, Kristen," Allison said, blushing.

"She might be in the Olympics someday," Beamer told me. "Allison's famous."

"Oh stop!" she said.

While they were talking, I just happened to glance into Allison's tote bag. In it was a copy of the newest I. M. Fine book, *The Ghost of Creepy Hollow*.

"Is that any good?" I asked, pointing to the book.

"What? Oh, yeah. It's great! Want to borrow it when I'm through?"

"No, thanks," I said. "Just curious."

"Let's get something to eat," Kristen said, gazing longingly at our burgers. "I'm starving."

"See you later," Allison said, and they headed over to the snack bar. Beamer gave me *the look* again.

"Can it, Beamer," I said. "All I did was ask if she liked the book."

"Right. No other thoughts passed through your mind."

"Give me a break! No thoughts passed through yours?"

"Yeah, okay, they did."

"So?"

"So. Eat your burger."

After consuming enough greasy food to choke a horse, followed by a fairly long argument over whether you really had to wait a full hour after eating before going into the pool (which I won, my argument being that getting *wet* didn't hurt you; it was just if you were actually *swimming* that you might get a cramp), we went into the water but stayed in the shallow end. The splashing and squealing was in full force by then.

Maybe because there was so much happy noise in the pool, we didn't hear the screams at first. But they were such a different kind of scream that I quickly became aware that something was wrong. I put my hand on Beamer's shoulder to get his attention.

"What *is* that?"

We both looked around, trying to figure out where it was coming from. Other people noticed, too. They stopped what they were doing and listened. An odd stillness fell over the crowd. We could hear it clearly then—it was a girl's voice, and the scream was one of sheer terror.

"Over there," Beamer said, pointing. "It's Allison."

Then I saw her. She was cowering against the chain-link fence, her hands up as if to protect herself from an attack. She was staring wildly in the direction of the snack bar and screaming hysterically. A couple of her friends were trying to calm her down, but she wasn't responding.

We pulled ourselves out of the pool and ran over to see if we could help.

"Allison, stop!" Kristen kept saying. "It's okay!"

"Make it go away!" she howled.

"What? Make *what* go away?"

Whatever it was, Allison obviously thought it was coming closer; she slid along the fence, then broke into a run.

"NO!" she screamed, running wildly, slamming into a picnic table, then plunging into the shallow end of the pool. I was scared she was going to hit her head, and obviously the lifeguard was, too, because he dove into the water instantly and went to her rescue. She wasn't hurt, though, except for a big scrape on her leg from the picnic table.

The lifeguard pulled her out of the pool and tried to calm her down.

"It's okay," he said. "Take it easy."

But Allison couldn't take it easy. She was terrified. She tried to break and run again, but the lifeguard stopped her.

"What?" he said, squeezing her arm. "What *is* it? Tell me!"

"Ggg . . . ghost," she said. And she waved her hands around, sort of indicating something gross dripping down from the ghost's face. The whole time, she kept her eyes plastered on the place where she thought it was standing. "It's all . . ." she muttered, her face a mask of horror and disgust, and then she screamed, "NO!" again, and practically burrowed into the lifeguard's armpit.

Somebody called 911, and in a few minutes an ambulance arrived. We all stood there in shock until it pulled away.

"I'm getting a little tired of seeing kids carted off in ambulances," I said.

"Yeah, me, too," Beamer agreed. "Let's go home."

In the car, the radio was playing classical music. I asked Mr. Gordon if we could switch to a news station.

"Sure," he said, and punched a button.

There was a very loud ad on, so I turned the volume down a little while Beamer told about how Allison

Simmons had lost her mind at the swimming pool.

"I hate to say this," Mr. Gordon said, "but it sounds like drugs."

"No way," Beamer said. "Not her."

"Well, I hope you're right," he said.

You could tell he didn't think there was any other possible explanation. I knew there was, though, and Beamer did, too.

The news came on again, so I turned it up. But it wasn't what I was expecting. Nothing about Allison at all. A pedestrian had been hit by a car on a residential street a few hours before.

"The victim, nine-year-old Trey Martin, is undergoing surgery at Harper's Mill Hospital. We believe that his injuries are minor, but we will give you an update as soon as information is available.

"The child apparently ran in front of a passing car driven by a neighbor, Hugo Reese. So far, no charges have been filed. According to witnesses, the boy seems to have suddenly panicked over something and started screaming and running toward the street. . . ."

I turned around and glared at Beamer in the backseat. He raised his eyebrows, then nodded. Creepy or not, he was with me now.

Allison was on the TV news that night, along with Trey Martin and two or three other kids who had been involved in strange incidents. One girl had tried to get out of her mother's car while they were going along the highway at about sixty miles an hour. Fortunately, she had trouble unhooking her seat belt, which gave her mother time to pull over. Except for Trey, who was recovering from surgery and in good condition, none of the kids had been seriously injured, and they all seemed to have regained their senses pretty quickly. But it could have been a whole lot worse.

Beamer switched to CNN. There was a reporter standing in the woods, with a crowd of people milling around in the background. He was interviewing a very tired-looking man in a Boy Scout leader's uniform. It seems that the evening before, his troop had been camping out, when suddenly one of the boys had become hysterical and run off into the woods. He had chased after this kid and caught him, but the boy was really wild and had to be restrained. The kid kept screaming that a ghost was after him. The scout leader denied that they had been telling ghost stories around a campfire or anything like that. They had just been cleaning up after dinner.

Anyway, while all this was going on, two more boys

went nuts, and then another and another. All of them thought they were being chased by something and ran like crazy to get away—all in different directions. This was a big problem, because there weren't enough Scout leaders to go after all the boys, and even when they caught hold of them, they kept trying to run away again. Plus, it was getting dark. One of the leaders used a cell phone to call the police.

After a while, most of the kids had come back, kind of confused and embarrassed. But one boy had gotten lost, and searchers had been out beating the woods for him all night. They had just found him about a half hour before. He was thirsty and scared, but otherwise okay.

This had happened, by the way, in Texas.

"Sounds like what happened to Allison," Mr. Gordon said.

"Yeah," we both agreed.

Neither of us was in the mood to stay up late that night, so not long after the Gordons went to bed, we did, too.

I went to the kitchen for a glass of ice water and was heading back down the hall to the guest room when Beamer peeked his head out of the study, where he was sleeping on the foldout couch.

"Franny," he said.

"What?"

"I was just thinking. Those books?"

"Yeah."

"Wouldn't they be printed in other countries, too?"

My heart sank. "Sure," I said. "Of course. Probably just about everywhere."

"Which means . . ."

"Yeah, Beamer," I said. "I know exactly what it means."

12

Wimberly, Pennsylvania, was a pretty place, in a quiet, old-fashioned way. You could tell the buildings lining the main street had been there for over a hundred years, maybe more. They had been modernized with big plate-glass windows and store signs, but that must have happened awhile back, because everything looked a little faded.

The bus had dropped us off at a corner on the town's main street. It was, to be precise, the corner of Maple and First, right in front of Starky's grocery. It is always important to pay attention to this kind of thing if you plan to find your way back. I'd learned this lesson the hard way, courtesy of my mom, the time she forgot where she had left her car at the airport.

"So where do you want to start?" Beamer asked.

"How about Starky's? Everybody has to buy groceries."

We went inside. It was a pretty shabby-looking place. The fluorescent bulbs flickered overhead and the linoleum was old and worn. There were two checkout counters, which seemed like one too many for this place. I guess the management thought so, too, because only one of them was open.

A young woman stood there chewing gum and studying her fingernails with fierce concentration. The nails were about two inches long—they had to be the kind you glue on, I decided—and they curved inward, like claws.

Beamer grabbed a Butterfinger and set it down in front of the cashier. Because of her long nails, she struggled to pick it up and run it over the scanner. Then she struggled some more to ring up the sale, flexing her hand so her fingernails wouldn't hit the wrong buttons on the cash register. Finally, she struggled to take Beamer's money and give him change. I caught Beamer staring in fascination. I gave him a poke in the ribs.

"Excuse me," I said in my most polite voice. "Could we ask you a question?"

She nodded.

"We're trying to find a children's book author named I. M. Fine. He lives here in Wimberly."

The name did not seem to ring a bell with her.

"I just thought maybe you might know him," I prompted. "Maybe he shops here."

"Sorry," she said. "Never heard of him."

"Why don't we see if he's listed in the phone book?" Beamer said. "Just for grins."

I was sure he wouldn't be, since he hadn't shown up on any of the Internet sites. Still, it was worth a try, just to cover all the bases. Maybe we'd turn up a relative.

"I guess we should," I agreed. "It would be pretty embarrassing if we looked all over town and then found out he was right there in the phone book." I looked up at the clerk and smiled sweetly.

"You'll have to ask the manager," she said, indicating the only other person in the store, a bald man in a dingy white apron who was taking canned peaches out of a box and putting them on the shelves.

The manager reluctantly stopped what he was doing and led us over to a cramped little office near the front of the building. He took out a ring of keys and unlocked the door, found a phone book, then stood there waiting while we looked for I. M. Fine in the white pages.

He wasn't there. No one else named Fine was,

either. I handed the book back to the manager and thanked him.

"That was great," Beamer said when we got outside. He broke the candy bar in two and gave me half. "Now what?"

"We just keep asking. If I. M. Fine still lives in Wimberly, somebody's bound to know him."

So we worked our way methodically down one side of the street and back up the other, asking everybody the same question. We asked at a drugstore, a bike shop, several clothing stores, a beauty shop, a pizza parlor, a shoe-repair shop, and a gas station. We went into a beer joint, but they told us we'd have to leave because we were underage. None of the people we talked to had ever heard of I. M. Fine.

By then, it was getting close to lunchtime and we were feeling frustrated, depressed, and hungry. So we stopped at a sub shop to get some sandwiches and restore our spirits.

"Okay, let's go about this logically," I said as we settled in to wait for our food. "I think we're talking to the wrong kinds of people. I mean, even if they saw I. M. Fine in their store every single week, they still might not know his name. And if they did, it would probably be as Isaac or Ivan or whatever, and they wouldn't take any special interest in him. Not if they don't know *who he is*—you know, that he's a famous author and all."

"Yeah, okay. So then who are the right people to ask?"

"Well, children, for starters—or their parents."

"That's good," he said. "And what about librarians or bookstore owners."

"Good. Who else?"

"I don't know—the candy factory?"

"Yeah, that's a possibility," I agreed. I was feeling better already.

The waitress arrived with our sandwiches. She looked old enough to have kids our age. Her name tag said JOANNE.

"Excuse me," I said, "but do you have kids?"

That turned out to be the magic question. Did she have kids? Of course she had kids! She gave us the first smile we had seen in Wimberly and settled in for what was obviously her favorite topic of conversation.

"I have three," she said. "Two big boys and a baby girl."

"That's great," I said. "Do they like to read?"

The waitress thought for a moment. "Well now, my oldest, Chris—he never was much of a reader. All he ever wants to do is play those video games. Such a waste of time is what I think, you know what I mean?"

I did, but I thought it best to keep the conversation on track. "Did Chris ever read the I. M. Fine books?

Lots of kids who don't read much still like them a lot."

"Oh, you mean those Chillers? Yeah, I think he read a couple. But my middle boy, Jason—now, he reads every single one of them. Buys them the minute they come out."

"Really!" we crowed in unison.

"Oh, yes. My Jason loves to read."

"Well, did you know that the author lives right here in Wimberly?"

She drew back in amazement. "Oh, you don't mean it!"

"Yes," I said. "It says so in his first book—'I. M. Fine lives in Wimberly, Pennsylvania.' Those are the very words."

"Well, I'll be! Jason will just be so thrilled to hear that."

"So I guess you've never met him or anything?" Beamer asked.

"Well, no," she said. "I didn't know he lived here until just this minute."

"The reason we were asking," he went on, "is that we're trying to interview him for a school project. Do you think anybody else here would know something about him? I mean, would you mind asking the other waitresses, maybe?"

"Well, sure, I could do that," she said, pulling our check out of her apron pocket and laying it on the table.

"I'll let you know if I find out anything." Then she headed back toward the kitchen.

"Well, that was refreshing," I said.

"We didn't learn anything, though."

"Maybe not. But she said she'd ask around. Don't get grumpy on me."

Beamer agreed not to get grumpy, and we settled in to eat our sandwiches. When we were ready to leave, we waved at Joanne. She came scurrying over.

"Any luck?" I asked.

"Oh, honey, no. But everyone was so impressed that we have a famous author living around here."

"Oh, well," said Beamer. "Thanks anyway."

I had a thought. "Can I ask you another question? I'm not trying to be nosy or anything; it's just part of our project."

"Well, sure, I don't mind."

"This is going to sound strange, but this past year, did your son—Jason—did he have a really bad headache that lasted for a couple of days?"

"He sure did. It was going around the school something awful."

"Did the other one . . ."

"Chris?"

"Right, Chris. Did he get it, too? Or the baby?"

"No, just Jason. I was terrified we'd all come down

89

with it, but he was the only one."

"And then, a few months later, did he have anything else happen? It was going around our school—sort of like seizures. Thrashing around on the floor, hissing—it was on the news."

"Oh, yes, I know what you're talking about."

"Well, did he? Did he have that?"

"Yes," she said, "lots of kids did." But she was squinting at us now like she wasn't sure why we were asking such strange questions.

"Well, the thing is," I explained, "we think those outbreaks were related to the books. The I. M. Fine books."

"No!"

"Yes! And that's actually why we're here. To investigate."

She shook her head in amazement. "Isn't that something!" she said.

One of the other waitresses called, "Joanne!"

"Sorry, kids, but I need to get back to work."

"Sure," I said. "Thanks for your help."

"You drop by later on, and I'll see what I can find out."

And she actually winked.

13

The library was next on our list. I just knew this was where we were going to hit pay dirt. You can count on librarians to know about books and authors.

But I quickly lost heart once we walked inside. The Wimberly library was a tiny storefront operation. I've seen convenience stores with more space. I've seen book-mobiles with more books.

"You want to apply for a library card?" asked the lady behind the desk.

"No," Beamer said. "We just have a question. About a local author."

She looked surprised. "Local author?"

"Yeah, the children's author, I. M. Fine. We heard he lives here in Wimberly."

"I. M. Fine?"

"He writes the Chillers series. Scary stories for kids."

"Oh, yes. I know the ones. I'm afraid we don't carry those books. We have a pretty limited budget."

"Well, actually, we were more interested in finding *him*," I said. "Here in Wimberly."

"Oh, well . . ." She looked truly regretful. "I'm afraid I can't help you there."

"Thanks anyway," Beamer said, and nudged me out the door.

He looked at his watch. "You know what, Franny? I'm starting to get nervous about this. What if my grandpa drives by the pool to check on us and finds out we're not there?"

"Oh, stop worrying, Beamer," I said. "He's in his garage, puttering with his inventions. I bet he hasn't given us a second thought."

"I don't know. I wouldn't put it past him to check."

"So if he does find out we left—which he won't—we'll just say we got bored and went for a walk."

"Give me a break! We went for a walk? All day?"

"He doesn't have to know how long we were gone—just why we weren't there at the exact moment he drove by."

"Okay, but what if he asks around at the pool? What if the lifeguard says, 'Yeah, I remember those two. They left twenty minutes after you dropped them off'?"

"Oh, all right," I said. I thought he was being a little paranoid, but I have to admit that asking an endless string of strangers if they had heard of I. M. Fine was getting a little stale.

So we headed back to Maple and First, stopping in at the occasional store on the way. As a result, we learned that I. M. Fine had failed to make himself known at Reynold's Hardware, the Tire Shop, Dunkin' Donuts, Hopwood Dry Cleaners, or the Five 'n' Dime.

The bus wasn't due for another half an hour, so we just stood there for a while, staring numbly up the road in the faint hope that it would come early and rescue us.

Suddenly, I had a thought. No matter how bummed out we were at the moment, we would still be coming back the next day. And it would speed things along if we had a plan. This led me to think of the candy company. I kind of liked the idea of trying something different from what we'd done so far. But we didn't have a clue where the candy company was.

I knew it couldn't be that hard to find out, though. After all, we were talking about a pretty big company. In fact, it was probably the biggest business in the whole town. I decided to pop into the barbershop and ask.

"Yell if you see the bus coming," I told Beamer. "I just want to check something out."

The barber was sitting in one of his two chairs, smoking a cigarette. There was not a customer in sight.

"Hello, little lady," he said.

I guess, being a barber, he didn't see a whole lot of females on a day-to-day basis, except maybe the mothers of six-year-olds who came in for a bowl cut. Still—*little lady?*

"Sorry to bother you," I said, "but I'm trying to find some information on a local company, the Kute Kandy Corporation. Do you know anything about it?"

"Kute Kandy," he said, shaking his head in disgust. "Can you imagine—a big company like that? Calling it Kute Kandy? The name's bad enough, but he had to spell it with a *K?*"

"Yeah, it does sound pretty silly," I said.

"It started out right over there," he said, pointing across the street to a dress shop. We had already been in there earlier that morning.

"Bermann's Candies, it was then. Little family business. I'll bet it employs three hundred people now. Maybe more. And he goes and calls it Kute Kandy!"

"The owner, you mean? Mr. Bermann?"

"Yeah, Jake Bermann. He's retired now. Moved to Florida."

"This is off the subject," I said, "but do you know the writer I. M. Fine? Lives here in Wimberly?"

"Fine?" He thought about it. "I knew an *Irving* Fine back in the early fifties. Or knew *of* him is more like it."

"Really?" I said, gasping. "Do you know where he lives?"

"Oh, sure," he said with a wicked grin. Even before he'd said it, I knew what was coming. "Yeah, he's been at the same address for quite some time. About six feet under. Headstone on top."

This guy was creepy, and I really wanted out of there, but I felt we were circling around something important.

"You said you knew *of* him. What exactly?"

"Well, little lady . . ." He leaned forward and paused dramatically. "He was a spy. A Russian spy."

"A spy!" I croaked. I had never heard of a real spy—just the movie kind, like James Bond.

The barber was still grinning. "Yes indeed, that's what he was."

"But how could you know a thing like that?" I asked. "He didn't tell you, did he?"

"Nope. I read it in the paper, same as everybody

else. Irving Fine was called down to Washington to testify about it. Gave our American secrets to the Russkies. So what do you think about that?" He raised his eyebrows to show how impressed I should be.

"Gosh," I said. "Did they put him in jail?"

"Should've. Didn't get a chance, though. Driving back from Washington—ka-blamm! Right into a telephone pole. It was in all the papers."

Well, this was plainly not our guy, but it might have been I. M. Fine's father. "Did he have a son, do you know?" I asked. "Like Irving, Jr., maybe?"

"Haven't got a clue," he said.

The bell tinkled and a teenage boy with hardly any hair came in and sat in the free chair. I couldn't imagine why he thought he needed a haircut. Maybe he wanted it all shaved off. The barber stubbed out his cigarette and got to his feet.

"Well, thanks," I said, edging toward the door. "Just one last thing. Do you know where in town, exactly, that candy factory is?"

"Kute Kandy." He said it again, just to enjoy how stupid it sounded. "Out on Route One. 'Bout two miles up the road."

"Route One?" I asked.

"Yeah, just head west, little lady—you'll see it. Over on the left."

"Thanks a lot," I said again, then got out of there as fast as I could.

Beamer didn't look like he had moved one millimeter since I'd been in the barbershop. He was still standing there, leaning against a lamppost, watching the northbound traffic.

"I found out where Kute Kandy is," I reported.

"Good." He didn't sound all that excited.

"But that's not all. It turns out there was an Irving Fine who lived here in the fifties. He's been dead for a long time, but Beamer—he was a spy!"

This time, Beamer actually turned and looked in my direction.

"He had to go to Washington for questioning or something. And on the way back, he was killed in a car wreck."

Beamer hit me with his laser gaze. "That's gotta be the father," he said.

"Yeah, that's what I thought. Fine isn't all that common a name."

"Plus, it kind of makes sense. I mean, with a dad like that, you might get kind of twisted. It fits, doesn't it?"

"Yes, it does."

And all of a sudden, my tiredness and frustration lifted and I positively couldn't wait till the next day arrived. We were going to find this guy. I just knew it.

14

The Kute Kandy Corporation wasn't as big as I'd expected it to be. I had just assumed that this factory made all the Jelly Bears and Jelly Worms and every other kind of Jelly whatnot in the whole world. But looking at the small cluster of buildings, I didn't think that was possible. I decided this was just the main office. They probably had lots of other factories in different places.

The main building was a big flat gray box with hardly any windows. Behind it, and off to the sides, were several other flat gray boxes, surrounded by miles of parking lot, full of cars and trucks.

We went through the double glass doors and into the reception area. I had expected something kind of nice— carpets on the floor, a shiny desk with a well-dressed receptionist sitting behind it, a few nice leather chairs to wait in.

Well, I was wrong. It was about as fancy as your neighborhood dry cleaners: linoleum floors, fake wood paneling, an old oak desk. There wasn't anybody sitting behind the desk, though, and there weren't any chairs to wait in, either—leather or otherwise.

"I think the receptionist must have gone to the ladies' room or something," I said. "I bet she'll be back in a minute." I had deduced this from the half-empty cup of coffee sitting on the desk. It had lipstick marks on the rim. Just call me Sherlock.

Within thirty seconds, a middle-aged woman appeared and took her place in the squeaky wooden chair behind the desk. "May I help you?" she asked.

"Well, yes," I stammered. "We wondered if there was somebody here we could talk to. About the history of the company."

She knitted her brows. If we had asked to hear the history of the dust ball under her desk, she couldn't have been more surprised.

"Like . . . what?" she said.

"Well, you know—like how Jake Bermann turned his little candy store into this big international company. Stuff like that."

She continued to gaze at us for a minute, the question "Why?" hovering on her lips. And in all fairness, why would anyone really want to explore the history of the Kute Kandy Corporation? Finally, she put on this really, really sorry look and said she was afraid there wasn't anybody around who could help us. "We don't have a public-relations person," she explained.

"How about someone older, who might have worked here for a long time?" Beamer suggested. "It could be anybody."

The woman sighed. She rubbed her eyes with her fingertips. She looked up at the ceiling. "I guess you could talk to Edna Franklin," she said with obvious reluctance. "But I don't think she can give you much time."

"Who is Edna Franklin?" I asked.

"She's Mr. Bermann's secretary." She was already dialing the number.

"Mr. Bermann?" I said, surprised. He was supposed to be in Florida.

The receptionist held up her hand, indicating that she couldn't talk to both me *and* Edna at the same time. I closed my mouth and waited while she explained our curious interest in the development of the Kute Kandy Corporation and asked whether Edna might be able to carve a few minutes from her busy schedule to answer our questions.

The conversation was short, but the upshot of it was that Edna agreed to see us. The woman directed us down the hall, first door to the right.

Edna was older all right. Her hair was as white as a cloud and her skin was almost as pale. Her blue eyes seemed to have faded along with the rest of her.

"Have a seat," she said politely.

We did.

"You want to know about the history of Kute Kandy?" she prodded.

"Well, sort of," I said. "That's part of it. Or, well . . ."

Come on, Franny, I thought. Get a grip. Edna waited patiently.

"We're actually trying to find someone who lives here in Wimberly. A famous author of children's books."

"Oh?"

"His name is I. M. Fine. He writes the Chillers series."

"Yes?" Her steady gaze made me squirm.

"Well, there is a connection with your company, actually. He wrote a book last year that featured Jelly Worms."

"Yes, I know about that."

"I guess you know that it started a fad. It was the in thing for kids to buy Jelly Worms for a while."

"I know," she said. "We had trouble filling all the orders."

"And your stock went way up," I said. "I know because my dad bought some."

"Yes, it did." She gave us a little smile.

"Well, anyway, he's the guy we're trying to find. We thought maybe since he put Jelly Worms in his story, he might have some connection with Mr. Bermann and the company. Maybe they are old friends or something."

Edna looked thoughtful, then shrugged her shoulders. "It's possible," she said. "Mr. Bermann has a lot of friends. He's a very kind man."

"Could we ask him?" I suggested.

"Oh," she said. "I was referring to Mr. Bermann, Sr. He's retired. He doesn't live in Wimberly anymore. It's his son who's president of the company now."

"Do you think the writer might be a friend of Mr. Bermann, Jr.?"

"Well, I doubt it. When we kept hearing about this book—this children's book about Jelly Worms—he was as perplexed as everyone else. Honestly, I don't think there's any connection. Our products are quite popular.

Anybody could put them in a book. It wouldn't have to be a friend of Mr. Bermann."

"So you don't know anything at all about I. M. Fine?" I asked desperately.

"The author, you mean?"

"Yes."

"Well, no. The only Fine I ever knew in Wimberly was Irving Fine, but he's been dead for many years."

"But you knew him—Irving Fine?"

"Yes, I knew Irving, though not very well. He was older, not part of my crowd. And, well, he came to a rather tragic end."

"He was a spy," I said. "That's what the guy in the barbershop said."

Edna heaved a great sigh. "He was accused of being a spy," she said. "That's true. It was a terrible, shocking thing. No one could believe it of him. To tell you the truth, I always thought that if he hadn't died when he did, if he'd had a fair trial, they would have found him innocent. But he didn't, of course. I guess you heard about the auto accident."

We both nodded.

"Well, anyway," Edna said, "a few years ago, after the Russians threw the Communist government out, the old files from the Cold War days were opened to the public. Can you imagine? All those famous old spy cases—now we could find out with absolute surety who the real traitors were!"

"And?"

"Irving was innocent. It was another man in his department who had sold the information to the Russians. It was in the papers, at least around here, but I guess some folks didn't see it—they still think of him as Wimberly's most notorious citizen."

"That's sad," I said.

"Yes," Edna agreed. "It is."

"Is there anything else you remember about him?" Beamer asked. "Did he have a family?"

"He was married, I know that much. He went to college in New York and he met his wife there."

"Did they have any kids?"

"Honestly, I can't tell you. I lost track of him when he went to New York. And like I said, he was quite a bit older than me."

"But he might have, don't you think?"

"Well, of course he might have."

"Is there anything else you remember? Anything at all?"

"Just that he was brainy, quite the academic star. Got a Ph.D. in—I don't remember exactly—physics, I think. Got a job teaching at the University of Pennsylvania. He was involved in some big government project. Very, very smart man."

"What about his wife? Did she stay in Wimberly after he died?"

"I don't remember anything about her, to tell you the truth—it was a long time ago. I would doubt it, though. Probably went back to her hometown. After something like that . . . who would want to stay?"

"Anything else you can think of?" I asked hopefully.

"No," she said. "I'm afraid not."

"Well, thanks for talking to us," I said, and got up to go.

"Now wait a minute," she said. "You haven't told me why you're so eager to find this writer."

I looked at Beamer, but he just gave one of those "Don't ask me" shrugs.

"Well, you see," I said, plunging in, "there's something about his books. They influence children like you wouldn't believe. Like with the Jelly Worms."

"Yes," she said.

"Only after that book, things sort of took a weird turn. We don't think he's good for kids. We want to talk to him. Maybe he doesn't really know he's hurting people."

"Well, well," she said. "Aren't you amazing! I sure wish I could help you."

She walked us to the door, a look of fierce concentration on her face. Then she stopped for a minute and seemed lost in thought. "You might check the old newspapers," she said. "See if you can find his obituary. It would have been around 1953, I think. The surviving family members would be listed. You could find out whether he had children or not. Maybe one of them is the writer you're looking for."

"Oh, thanks," I said. "That's a great idea!"

She stood there in the doorway, smiling, and watched us as we headed back down the hall. As we turned the corner, I looked back at her and she waved.

"Good luck," she said.

15

We had convinced the bus driver to drop us off at the candy factory that morning, since the bus route ran right past it. It hadn't seemed all that far from town. But now that we had to walk back, it seemed really, really far. Plus, there were no sidewalks, only the shoulder of the highway, which was narrow and dusty, not to mention dangerous. We had to walk in single file most of the way, with cars whizzing past us like rockets.

We reached town at last, a lot dustier and sweatier than when we'd started.

"I need food," Beamer said. "And something wet, with ice in it. And I want to sit down."

We were near the sub shop. It had all of those things. Plus, we had asked the waitress, Joanne, to ask around about I. M. Fine. It wouldn't hurt to check. Maybe something had turned up.

We went inside and took a booth. A waitress came over to take our order, but it wasn't Joanne. We asked if she was there.

"Yeah," our waitress said. "You want me to send her over?"

We said we just needed to ask Joanne a question. No hurry. Whenever she had a free minute. But in the meantime, could we please have two supersubs, some chips, and two Cokes? She said we could and went off to get them.

"So how are we going to do this?" Beamer asked. "They're not going to have old newspapers in the Wimberly library. So where do we go? Philadelphia? And then what? Read every single newspaper they published in 1953? And what if it's not 1953? It might be 1952 or 1954. Like, we're going to read nine hundred papers cover to cover?"

"On microfilm," I said.

"What?"

"It's bound to be on microfilm, don't you think? That's how they always do it in libraries. Newspapers would be too bulky to keep; plus, newsprint falls apart. We'll have to read it on one of those little light-box dealies."

"Oh, great. That makes it even more fun."

"Maybe somebody at the library could help us. Like, say, the obituaries are always on the back page or something. Or maybe there's some kind of an index."

"It's going to take weeks, you know that?"

"Or we might get lucky."

"Like we've been lucky so far?"

"Yeah," I said. "Like that."

"Hi there, you two!" It was Joanne. Her hands were on her hips and she was smiling. "I was hoping you'd come back."

My heart leapt. "Really?" I said. "Did you find something out?"

"Well, I think so. Mind if I sit down?"

"Oh, yes—please!"

We both jumped to our feet. Beamer grabbed a chair from a nearby table and swung it over for Joanne. She sat down and sighed with relief.

"Feels good to get a load off," she said.

"I'll bet," Beamer said.

"Well, okay—you two look like you're about to bust a gasket, so calm down and I'll tell you what I heard. I got it from my mother-in-law, and she's a little confused sometimes, so you need to take it all with a grain of salt."

"All right, go ahead."

"Well, there was this guy who lived here some time

ago; Irving Fine was his name. There was some kind of scandal about him. . . ."

"Yeah, we know all about that," Beamer interrupted. "They thought he was a spy."

"Really!" Joanne looked genuinely shocked. "Well, Mimi didn't say what the scandal was about. A spy! Really?"

"Yeah, except he wasn't really—it was all a big mistake. Did Mimi say anything else?" I was praying it wasn't going to be the same old story, third version.

"Well, he died," Joanne said kind of sweetly, as if she were breaking the news to near relatives.

"Yeah, we heard that, too. Do you know anything about his family?"

"Well, I was just getting to that," she said, leaning forward conspiratorially. "Mimi says that one of that man's kids lives up at the old Calloway place on Pleasant Hill Road. She feels sure the name is Fine, same as the father."

"No kidding," I said, almost breathless with excitement.

"That's what Mimi said. Mildred Calloway was an aunt or something. She's been gone for a good long time now. My mother-in-law used to know everybody's business in this town—that's how come I asked her. I mean, she knew *everything*! I suspect there are a few folks in town who are relieved her memory is starting to drift—if you know what I mean."

"She didn't tell you the name? Of Irving Fine's child?"

"No, Mimi was more interested in talking about Irving Fine and how he scandalized the whole town. Refused to tell me what he'd done, though. I thought he'd run away with the preacher's wife or something. Tell you the truth, I think Mimi couldn't quite call it to mind."

Our waitress brought the subs. Joanne looked up and gave the waitress a big smile and a motherly pat on the arm.

"I'm almost done, hon," she said.

"Don't worry about it," the waitress assured her. "We're not busy."

"So anyway, that's pretty much all I found out. I expect you could just hop on over there and ring the bell. Writers work at home most times, don't they?"

"Yeah, I guess so. But we'll need the address."

"Oh, gosh. I don't have the number, but I can draw you a map. It won't be hard to find."

She pulled a pen out of her apron and grabbed a napkin.

"Okay, now you kids walking?"

"Yes."

"Well, it'll be a bit of a hike. But what you want to do is head down Maple that way"—here she indicated the direction with her right hand—"then hang a left on Scenic Road."

She drew a curving line on the napkin and labeled it in block letters.

"You'll stay on Scenic for a good long way and it will curve around and start heading up the hill. Then you want to start looking for Pleasant Hill Road and you'll go right."

She drew a little box to represent the Calloway house. She put an X in it.

"The house is going to be on the left-hand side, about halfway up the road. There's kind of a park across from it—nice trees and grass and all. The house is a gray Victorian type with frilly iron stuff along the roof. Needs a paint job."

"Does it look different from the other houses around there? So we don't go to the wrong place. . . ."

"It's the only one that's gray, I'm pretty sure. And it's not as fixed up, if you know what I mean. My kids used to think it was haunted. See, Pleasant Hill is one of those neighborhoods that used to be really ritzy—like back in Mildred Calloway's time—but then it sort of went downhill for a while. People with money wanted new houses, you know, with central heat and all. Then it came back in fashion again to have these antique houses and spruce them up. Very Martha Stewart, you know. Only not this one. I don't think you can miss it."

"Wow—thank you so much," I said. "You really have no idea—we've been dragging all over town for two days and we thought we were going to have to spend the rest of the summer reading old newspapers. And now we can just pop on up there. . . ."

"Not 'pop.'" Beamer said. "Trudge."

"Well, fine, we can just trudge on up there and get this thing over with."

Joanne heaved herself to her feet.

"Well, I hope this doesn't mean we won't be seeing you again. I've kinda taken a shine to the both of you."

"We'll come to visit," I promised, though I knew we probably wouldn't. Joanne was one of those people you meet, then never see again—but who stays in your memory forever.

"You tell Jason to stay away from those I. M. Fine books," I said "Especially the next one."

"I'll do that, hon."

16

Joanne had been right. The old Calloway house stuck out like a sore thumb. All the other houses on the block were totally fixed up, with potted geraniums and old-fashioned porch swings and bright green shutters. And right in the middle of all that new paint and cuteness stood this dark, faded, shabby old house.

I don't want you to think this was one of your typical haunted houses, with shutters hanging off at an angle and broken windows and all. It wasn't *that* bad. It just felt—I don't know—sad.

I turned to Beamer. "Are we ready for this?" I asked. "Do we know what we're going to say?"

"Well, not really. I mean, we can't exactly plan it till we get a feel for the situation. Like if he's angry or seems dangerous, then we need to take one approach. If he invites us in for milk and cookies, then that's another story."

"I'd be more worried about the milk and cookies," I said. "Isn't that how child molesters work?"

"You're saying we shouldn't go in the house? Even if he invites us in?"

"Well, I don't know. But I think we ought to talk about it now, before we go up there."

"Can't we just play it by ear?" Beamer suggested.

"What do you mean?"

"Well, like if he turns out to be some muscular hulk that could overpower us, then we probably want to stay outside. Maybe just talk on the porch. But if he's some wizened little old guy with a cane—well then, the two of us can probably handle him."

"Okay," I said. "That makes sense."

"But how do we open this conversation? 'Hi! We think you're evil'?"

"Yeah, that's good."

"Franny . . ."

"Sorry. Okay—how about this? We start out by apologizing for bothering him. I mean, he's really gone out of his way to protect his privacy, so I don't think he's going to be all that happy when we come knocking on his door. So let's say we're very, very sorry to bother him and we know how busy he is—and then we can try a little flattery. You know, how he's so famous and people must always be wanting his autograph. Like that."

"Right, at which point he slams the door."

"Fine, Beamer. Let's hear your version."

"I say we hit him between the eyes. Like we're the FBI. Tell him we know what he's up to and we plan to make him stop. That we'll be watching and if he ever does it again, we'll tell the police. And I think we should say we left a note at home, to be opened in case we don't come back, telling where we went and why. That way, he won't kill us, thinking he can cover up his crime."

"*Kill us!* Beamer, you watch too much TV."

"I do not."

"Look, here's what we should do. We'll start out my way and end up your way. Only a little nicer. We're not a SWAT team here, Beamer. We don't want to look totally stupid."

"All right," he said, throwing up his arms in exasperation. "Let's get this over with."

The house sat high on the lot. To reach the front door, we walked up a sloping sidewalk with a few steps placed at intervals, then up more steps to the porch. From there, we could see out past the green space across the street to the town of Wimberly spread out below.

Despite the great view, the house itself was pretty run-down—a lot worse than it looked from the street. The paint on the porch floor was peeling and the white trim was dirty and stained. There was a yellow sign nailed to the door frame: NO SOLICITORS, it said.

Beamer rang the bell. We waited a full minute, but nobody came to the door.

"Shouldn't we knock?" I suggested. "Maybe the bell's broken."

"Keep your shirt on," he said. "I heard a dog barking."

We waited another minute. I was just about to knock, when I heard a shuffling sound on the other side of the door and the click of a dead bolt being turned. Then the door opened about six inches, held fast by a safety chain.

Peering out at us was a woman, very gaunt and pale, with short, frizzy red hair. Her eyes were electric blue.

"What do you want?" the woman said.

"We need to speak with I. M. Fine," Beamer explained. "We won't take long, I promise. But it's very important."

"You have the wrong house," she snapped, and shut the door.

I looked at Beamer and Beamer looked at me.

I knocked again. The door opened immediately. The woman must have been standing there, waiting for us to leave.

"Will you please get off my property?" she said.

"I'm really sorry," I said, trying to sound harmless and sweet, "but we must have gotten bad directions. Do you know which house he lives in?"

"No, I don't. And I would like you to go now."

"Okay," we said in unison, and scurried off the porch and down the hill like a pair of terrified rabbits.

We stood in the park area, gazing up at the house.

"Okay," I said. "Here's the big question: Who the heck *is* that woman?"

"You don't think we just got the wrong house?"

"Well, I mean maybe . . . but it matches Joanne's description."

"He might have moved."

"Yeah, but if that's the case, why didn't she say so?"

"I don't know, Franny."

"I think he's there and she didn't want us to know."

"Why not?"

"Well, you remember that Stephen King movie we saw on TV? About the writer who is held hostage by a crazy fan?"

"Yeah—with Kathy Bates."

"Well, what if that lady is keeping I. M. Fine a prisoner in there?"

"You know what, Franny? You watch too much TV."

"Oh, shut up, Beamer. Let's concentrate."

"I am concentrating. And what I think is, we need to stop it with the wacko theories and find out whether he actually lives in that house or not."

"It was not a wacko theory," I said. "But okay, I agree that is the key question. So maybe we should ask the neighbors. . . ."

But Beamer wasn't listening to me. He was gazing up the street, with his eyes bright and his mouth hanging open.

"What?" I said, following his gaze.

And then I saw it, too. Happy days! Here came the mailman.

"Are you thinking what I'm thinking?" he asked.

"Yes, I am—only . . . isn't it against the law?"

"What?"

"Tampering with the U.S. mail."

"Who's tampering? I just want to see who the mail's addressed to."

"Yeah, so do I."

We waited until the postman put the letters into the

mailbox. I decided that if the lady came out and got her mail before we could sneak up and look at it, I would chase down the mailman and ask him. But she didn't. We sat there in the shadow of the trees and watched for a full ten minutes, and no one came out.

"She probably doesn't know the mail has arrived," I said. "If we're going to do it, we need to do it now."

"What if she's watching out the window?"

"Then she would have seen the mailman."

"Yeah. All the same," Beamer said, "let's go up to the blue house and cut over to the porch from the side. It won't be so obvious."

I agreed. We got as far as the flower bed, then turned and headed across the lawn to the gray house. We ducked down slightly as we came around the side of the porch, then tiptoed up the steps.

"Let's do this quickly and get out of here," I whispered.

Beamer nodded silently. He reached up and opened the mailbox. He pulled out a few letters and some catalogs. Then Beamer held out an envelope for me to see, a huge smile on his face.

It was a bill from the telephone company and it was addressed to I. M. Fine.

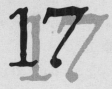

N ow what?" Beamer said.

We were back down at the park, having repeated our scampering rabbit routine a second time. I was too breathless and excited to answer for a minute. I put my hand over my heart and took some slow, deep breaths.

"Okay," I said, "let's think this through. What did we find out? First: I. M. Fine *does* live there. And second: The lady who answered the door said he *didn't* live there. So she was lying. Am I right so far?"

"Right."

"Now she wouldn't have any reason to lie unless she was covering something up—do you agree with that?"

"No. I think she's probably his wife or his house-keeper or something, and she was just trying to make us go away."

"But why would she tell us we had the wrong house? Wouldn't she just say, 'Mr. Fine is too busy to see fans'—something like that?"

"Well, most people would. Maybe she thought it was easier to lie."

"I don't buy it, Beamer. I like my original theory."

"What—that I. M. Fine is being kept a prisoner up there?"

"Yes. And Beamer, before you jump down my throat and tell me I'm crazy, just remember that you thought I was crazy when I said that his books were giving kids headaches."

"That doesn't make you right all the time, Franny."

"Yes, I know that. But listen—there's more to it. Like how do you explain this guy writing books for years and years and they don't affect kids in any special way—and then all of a sudden, this year, they turn toxic?"

"I don't."

"Well, I do. I think that lady has him locked in the basement or something and is making him write those bad books."

Beamer rolled his eyes, then sighed.

"Even if your theory is right, Franny, what are we supposed to do about it?"

I thought for a minute.

"Well, we could wait till she goes out. Then see if we can sneak into the house and, you know, rescue him."

"No way!"

"Okay, Beamer. How about we just peek in the windows? See what we can find out."

Beamer shook his head. "I don't know," he said.

"Well, then, let's hear *your* big idea."

"Obviously, Franny, I haven't got one. We'll wait."

And we did—for about two hours. I actually fell asleep there for a while. Fortunately, Beamer didn't, because he poked me and whispered, "Franny! There's a car backing down the driveway!"

I sat up and watched. The driver was our lady all right. And as far as I could tell, she was alone.

"Let's go," I said.

We hurried back up the hill. There was an iron gate at the entrance to the backyard, but all we had to do was slide a little bolt and push. I don't think anyone had opened it in a while, because it was stiff and creaky and didn't open all the way. We squeezed through, then followed a stone path along the side of the house to the garden.

It must have been beautiful once. High hedges surrounded it and a stone fountain stood in the center. At the fountain's edge was a statue of a fish rising up on its tail and opening its mouth really wide. That was probably where the water was supposed to come out, only there wasn't any water anymore, just moldy leaves. Around the fountain, there were stone walks alternating with flower beds, all of them full of weeds.

"Wow!" I said. "It's like the secret garden!"

"The what?"

"*The Secret Garden*. It's a book. About this man whose wife had this beautiful garden, and she loved it so much, she spent all her time there. Then one day, she fell off a tree branch and died. And so after that, the man hated the garden and he shut it up, and no one went in there for years and years and everything withered and died. Then two kids came along and found it and brought it back to life!"

"Hmm. Okay."

"Never mind, Beamer. Let's have a look."

We crept up the back porch and peered through the glass top of the kitchen door. There was a lot of reflection on the glass, so it was kind of hard to see. But I could tell the kitchen was really big and kind of old-fashioned-looking. Not like in olden times, with butter churns and woodstoves—more like a kitchen from the fifties. It was tidy, though. No dishes lying around or anything.

I opened the screen door and tried the knob. It was locked, naturally. I closed the screen door again, then turned to look for Beamer.

He was leaning over and looking into a window. I mean right *into* the window.

"Beamer! It's open?"

"Yeah. Sounds pretty quiet in there," he whispered. "I don't hear any prisoners screaming."

I went over and pushed the window up farther.

"Oh no you don't!" Beamer said. "We agreed to look in through the windows—not break and enter."

"No breaking necessary," I said, hoisting myself up over the sill and through the window headfirst. "You can stay out there if you want."

I found myself draped across the kitchen counter—a sort of ugly linoleum with a design of yellow-and-gray squares. I had to move a couple of pots of herbs before I could get my legs through and turn around.

"Are you out of your mind?" Beamer hissed though the window.

"I guess," I whispered back. "Yell if you see her coming."

I looked around the room. The main kitchen door was open, and I could look through and see all the way down the hall to the front of the house. There were three other doors in the kitchen as well, not counting the one to the backyard. I checked them out, one by one. The first was a pantry and the next one was a broom closet. The third opened on to a hallway and a set of stairs.

I knew what those were—the back stairs. Lots of old houses had them. My grandmother said that in the old days when rich people had servants who lived in the house, the servants used the back stairs to come and go from their bedrooms.

The stairs were dark, but I didn't think it would be smart to switch on the lights. So I climbed slowly and carefully, hanging on tightly to the banister. At the top landing, I looked around. It wasn't as dark up there, because the doors to the rooms were open and, of course, the rooms had windows. I knew right away there was nobody there—it was just too quiet. It had an untouched feel, and I could tell at a glance that the rooms were being used for storage. Still, I looked into each one just to be thorough.

I returned to the kitchen. Beamer was still looking through the window with a horrified expression on his face.

"Franny," he whispered, "that is so against the law!"

"Yeah, I know," I said. "But I'm doing it anyway, so stop bugging me."

"Franny."

"What?"

"At least unlock the back door so you can get out fast if you need to."

"Good thinking," I said.

I decided to try the basement next. I knew some basements had entrances from the backyard, with these big metal doors you pull up. But I hadn't seen one outside, so I figured that there would be an inside door. Remembering my grandmother's house, I decided to look under the back stairs.

This time, I turned on the light in the little hall off the kitchen. And sure enough, on the long wall at the side of the stairs, there was a door.

It felt a lot creepier opening that door than it had going upstairs. I told myself there was no logical reason for this, took a deep breath, and turned the knob.

I felt a wave of cold, damp air pass over me. With it came a musty smell. The only light I saw was a bare bulb hanging above the landing of a crude wooden staircase. I thought, What the heck! and pulled the chain.

It was just a regular basement—dusty and cold and full of pipes and spiderwebs. I shut the door and went back to the kitchen again.

"Well?" Beamer whispered. "Are you satisfied?"

"Nothing in the back rooms. Nothing in the basement. I'm going to try the front of the house now."

"If the police come, Franny, I'm out of here."

"Fine!" I said, and crept very softly down the front hall.

The dining room, on my right, was dark, the velvet drapes on the windows tightly shut. It looked like nobody had eaten in there for about a hundred years.

Across the hall from it was a large living room. I could see that the lights were on, so I peeked around the door frame very carefully. Nobody there, either. But someone had been in there not too long ago. There were books and newspapers scattered around and a coffee mug on the end table by the armchair.

It was an elegant room, with antique furniture and a marble fireplace with built-in mahogany bookshelves on either side of it. The books looked old, their spines kind of dark and faded. But I saw something in the far corner of the bookcase that caught my eye—a whole string of paperback books in bright modern colors. I knew what they were from across the room: the complete works of I. M. Fine.

I went over and took one off the shelf. It was number seventeen, *Grave's End.* The cover showed a graveyard with all sorts of really awful, partially decomposed bodies rising up out of the dirt. I put it back. The books, I saw by the series numbers on the spines, had been neatly arranged in order of publication.

I looked around for anything else of interest. There was a desk at the back of the room, so I went over to check it out. I saw bills and papers arranged in neat piles, and I was just noting the fact that there was no sign of a computer or typewriter when I heard the soft tread of footsteps in the hall. Frantically, I looked for a place to hide. I dashed across the room and ducked down behind the couch.

The footsteps came closer. Then I saw the shoes. They were Beamer's shoes. I stood up.

"Cheez, Beamer! You scared me."

"I couldn't stand waiting out there any longer," he said. "But please—let's hurry and do this and get the heck out of here."

"Look," I said grabbing his wrist and dragging him over to the bookcase. "They're all here. Organized by number."

"Sweet," he said. "So I guess there isn't any doubt, is there?"

"Not a shred. Come on. Let's look upstairs."

"After you," he said.

The first bedroom we came to was obviously the woman's. There were personal things on the dresser, like lotions and perfume, and there was a pair of ladies' shoes on the floor. The closet was full of women's clothes—and only women's clothes.

I wondered what that meant, exactly. I mean, if the lady was I. M. Fine's wife, wouldn't they be sharing the same room? And if she was his housekeeper, it would be odd for her to get the master bedroom.

Beamer signaled for me to keep moving.

There was a smaller room down the hall. It was furnished with twin beds in matching white chenille bedspreads. It was perfectly neat, but there was a layer of dust over everything. This place was starting to remind me of Sleeping Beauty's castle.

Finally, we tried the third room. Like the master bedroom, it faced the front of the house and had a nice view of the park. It had been made into a home office, with a computer, a printer, filing cabinets, a copier, and a fax machine. There were reading glasses and an empty Coke can on the desk.

I noticed a faint smell in the air. It seemed familiar. What was it?

And then I realized. It was perfume. I had smelled it in the bedroom.

"Beamer," I said, "I was wrong. That lady isn't keeping I. M. Fine a prisoner here."

"No?"

"Because, Beamer, that lady *is* I. M. Fine."

18

I pulled open the filing cabinet to the left of the chair. Inside were book files, neat as pins, the titles carefully lettered on the green-and-yellow tabs in dark blue ink. They were all there: *The Worm Turns*, *Mind Wave*, *Sinister Serpent Surprise*, *The Ghost of Creepy Hollow*, and, right in front, a new book, *The Avenging Word*.

I pulled out the file and sat down to look it over while Beamer went through the other filing cabinet. He was muttering under his breath. Something about the police and going to jail.

"Oh, stop being such a weenie, Beamer," I said.

The first thing in the file was a manuscript with "*The Avenging Word*, by I. M. Fine" typed on the cover sheet. Down at the bottom, it said "Riverbend Press,

Inc." The manuscript was pretty thick—more than a hundred pages. After that, I found a contract.

AGREEMENT: Between Ida May Fine (hereinafter referred to as "the Author") and Riverbend Press, Inc., a New York corporation having its principal place of business at . . ."

"Beamer, look at this!" I said, really excited. "I was right! Her real name is Ida May Fine."

Beamer was sitting cross-legged on the floor, studying a file of his own. He looked up and nodded but seemed more interested in what he was reading.

"What's that? What've you got?" I asked.

"A file—named 'Doomsday.'"

"Doomsday!"

"Yup."

"Yikes, Beamer. That sounds scary. What's in there?"

"It's a will. Here—look."

I put the contract for *The Avenging Word* back into the file and put the file away. Then I took the paper from Beamer.

It was a single page. Not a regular legal document like the contract, just typed on the computer.

THE LAST WILL AND TESTAMENT OF IDA MAY FINE

It is my desire, at the time of my death, that all my worldly goods, including the money, stocks, and other investments in my two accounts at Merrill Lynch, my house at 1407 Pleasant Hill Rd., Wimberly, PA, with all its contents, plus any future income from the sale of my books, be used for the support of my dog, Jake—should he still be living at the time of my death—in the utmost comfort for the rest of his natural life.

"Wow, Beamer! Can you believe that? She wants to leave her fortune to her dog!"

"So what have you got against dogs?"

"Nothing, Beamer. But cheez . . ."

"Keep reading, Franny. The clock's ticking."

"Okay. Right."

After Jake's death, I don't really care what you do with the remainder of my estate, with one proviso. I have videotaped a speech, which I wish to have broadcast widely throughout the country. This will probably require the purchase of commercial time on television stations nationwide. The executors of my estate are to spend whatever is necessary to assure that the maximum number of viewers is reached. After that, they can get their greedy hands on my money to their hearts' content. It won't really matter one way or another.

The will was signed and notarized at the bottom.

"Man, that is one bitter lady," I said.

"And here it is," Beamer said, holding up a videotape. "This was in the file, too."

"Great! I saw a TV in the bedroom. Maybe she has a VCR, too."

"You want to stay here and watch a video? Are you totally out of your mind? Franny, she could come home any minute!"

"But this could be important! It could be evidence!"

"Then let's take it. We'll watch it at home."

Beamer looked at his watch. "Oh, cripes!" he said. "It's almost four-thirty. We'll never get back before my grandpa goes to the pool to pick us up."

"Call him and say we were invited over to a friend's house. We're having dinner there and we'll get a ride home."

"How are we going to manage that? The ride home?"

"I don't know, Beamer. Just call."

I handed him the phone. He set it on the floor between his legs and punched in the number.

"Hi, Grandpa?" Beamer said. "Sorry to interrupt you, but . . ."

He told his story pretty convincingly, I thought. He even made up a name for this imaginary friend who had invited us over for dinner—Marshall. I wondered where the heck that had come from. I'd never met anyone named Marshall in my whole life.

I was standing there listening to his end of the conversation and looking around at the stuff in I. M. Fine's office when I thought I heard the clunk of a car door shutting.

"Beamer!" I whispered, waving at him wildly to get his attention. "Hang up!"

"Grandpa?" he said. "Marshall's mom needs to use the phone now. See you tonight."

"What?" he asked, scrambling to his feet.

"A car door. It might not be her, but we need to get downstairs—now!"

We crept out onto the landing and started down the stairs.

Just then, I heard the back door slam. I heard footsteps in the kitchen. I heard a dog bark.

"Oh no, Beamer—the dog!"

Suddenly, the dog was running up the hall to the front of the house, his tags jingling, his nails tapping on the hardwood floor. Then there he was at the bottom of the stairs, looking up at us. He was a medium-sized dog, not any regular breed. He had black fur everywhere, except for his floppy ears and long, pointed nose, which were honey brown, and his feet, which were white. He looked like a very nice dog. Just as I was thinking this, he began barking ferociously and dashed up the stairs like he wanted to rip our throats out.

"Quick!" I said, grabbing Beamer's sleeve and pulling him back toward the unused bedroom. We got there just before Jake did.

Jake clawed at the door and barked. I could hear Ida May coming up the stairs. "Jake?" she was calling, "What's the matter, boy?"

"In the closet," Beamer hissed. "Now!"

The closet wasn't very big and it was full of winter clothes and extra shoes. We managed to get inside and shut the door.

"You still have the tape?" I whispered.

"Yes," Beamer said. Outside, the dog was barking steadily and beating on the bedroom door.

"Stop it, Jake," I heard Ida say. "You be a good dog."

But Jake kept whining and clawing at the door. "What?" Ida said. Her voice was really close now. Then she must have opened the door, because Jake thundered into the bedroom and ran straight for the closet. He was sniffling at the crack under the door, inches from my feet. I squeezed Beamer's arm.

Ida was quiet for a minute while Jake used his most eloquent dog language to tell her that there were intruders inside that closet, sitting on her winter shoes. The quiet was ominous. It meant that she knew we were in there—well, she knew *someone* was in there—and she was trying to decide which of several unpleasant things to do about it.

Suddenly, the door swung open and Jake was in our faces, barking. I was too scared of the dog to look at Ida; I just put my arm across my face and curled up into a ball.

"Good, Jake! That's a nice dog. Yes, you're such a pretty boy. . . . Yes, you are." This was Beamer, dog lover of the world. Jake was putty in his hands. I sat up and saw Beamer stroking the dog, who was sniffing him in a friendly way and licking his arms and face. With his other hand, Beamer passed the tape to me behind his back.

Ida was standing there with her arms crossed, glaring at us with a mixture of rage and curiosity.

"Nice doggy," Beamer said.

"You stay right where you are," Ida said, her voice like ice. "Because I'm going to call the police." She pointed at the dog and backed toward the door. "Stay, Jake!" she said.

Beamer was still petting Jake and muttering sweet endearments. The minute Ida was out of the room, we made a dash for it, down the stairs to the front hall. Even with the time it took us to unlock the door and free the safety latch, we were still faster than Ida. We were down the sidewalk and into the park in seconds.

I looked back then, just before we plunged in among the trees and bushes. Ida stood there on the front porch, one hand shielding her eyes from the light, her hair glowing like fire in the afternoon sun.

19

Getting home was a nightmare. We were covered with mud and scratches from cutting through the park. We had to huddle in the doorways of nearby shops while waiting for the bus—which took forever—because we were afraid a police car might drive by and spot us. Then, by the time we finally made it back to Harper's Mill, the pool was closed and we couldn't get our tote bag. So we cleaned up as best we could in the bus station rest room, then walked all the way back to the house.

I felt really ragged. I was tired from our great escape and the long walk. And being scared had done something strange to my body chemistry. Floating over all that was a dark cloud of guilt.

The fact is, I'm not cut out for a life of crime. I had to keep reminding myself that we had done what we did for a good reason. Ida May Fine had caused Allison to throw herself into a swimming pool and those Boy Scouts to get lost in the woods—not to mention sending my sister to the hospital. And she had more tricks up her sleeve. We were just trying to stop her. You can't make an omelette without breaking eggs.

I let Beamer make up a story for his grandparents about playing touch football in Marshall's backyard and getting all scratched up. Actually, I didn't hear the whole thing. I disappeared into the guest room, tossed the video onto the bed, and took a long, hot bath. I guess I sort of lost track of the time, because after a while I heard Mrs. Gordon's voice outside the door, asking if I was all right. "Just tired," I said.

I emerged from my bath a little more relaxed and a lot cleaner than when I had gone in. I got dressed and went to look for Beamer.

I found him at the computer, checking his e-mail. He had made a huge bowl of popcorn, and now he was alternately scarfing it down, licking the butter and salt off his fingers, and typing on the keyboard.

"Eeew, gross, Beamer," I said, grabbing a handful of popcorn for myself.

"I was starving," he said by way of explanation.

"Yeah. Too bad we ate at Marshall's."

"What did you do with the video?" he asked, closing out the e-mail program and leaning back in the chair with another handful of popcorn.

"In my room," I said. "On the bed."

"I think we ought to wait till they're really and truly asleep before we play the tape."

"Yeah, I agree. So what do you think's on there?"

"Who knows?" Beamer said. "I hope it's a confession, because then we can just take it to the police."

I sighed. "I've been thinking about that. You know, that tape wouldn't be admissible in court. The police couldn't use it."

Beamer turned and stared at me. "Why not?"

"I saw it on *Law and Order*. We stole the tape, Beamer. We broke into her house and stole it. You have to have a search warrant to look for evidence in a person's house."

Beamer gave me a stricken look. "You mean we did all that for nothing? Practically got ourselves arrested?"

"No. Not for nothing. We found out a whole lot, and the tape is going to tell us more. I mean—the message she wants to give the world after her death? It has to be important."

"Yeah, but if we can't take it to the police, then we're just exactly where we were when we started. We may know more, but we're not any closer to stopping her. Plus, we can't go back and talk to her again, because she'll call the cops."

"I know," I said. "We need a different approach. And here's what I was thinking in the bathtub: Let's say you overheard DeeDee saying she had some evil plans—she was going to blow up the school or something. What would you do?"

"DeeDee blowing up the school? That's pretty far-fetched."

"Don't worry about whether it's realistic. Just tell me what you'd do."

"I don't know—call her parents, I guess."

"Exactly. Tell her family. If we could find one of Ida's relatives, then maybe they could stop her before things get really out of hand. And if the tape is as good as we think it's going to be, we can use it to convince them we're not making this up."

"Franny, she may not have any family. Her dad is dead—we know that—and her mom probably is, too. I mean, Ida left her money to her dog, remember?"

"True. But that may not mean anything. Her mom might still be alive, only Ida didn't put her in the will because she's so much older. Or maybe Ida's just crazy about animals. We're talking about a pretty twisted person here."

Beamer scraped up a handful of half-popped kernels from the bottom of the bowl. It sounded like he was cracking his teeth as he chewed them.

"Even so," he said (*crunch, crunch*), "how would we find these relatives?"

"I'm getting to that—Irving Fine's obituary! It'll have the mother's name and Ida's brothers' and sisters', too, if she has any. Once we get the names, we can look them up on the web."

"You want to spend the next two weeks in the library?"

"Well, actually, I was thinking we could try that website we found last spring. Remember? That one where you can spy on your neighbors?"

"That's for people who are alive, Franny. Not people who died fifty years ago."

"Are you sure? Don't people use the Internet to look up their family trees and stuff? Great-uncle Henry who died out in California during the gold rush?"

"I think that's something different. But if you really want, we could try."

After about twenty minutes of fruitless surfing, we

found a site called Superspy.com. It wasn't the one we'd found before, but it had tons of options: a Regular Search for $12.95, a Supersearch ("Regularly $39.95! Right now, half price!"), and an Exhaustive Super-search for $47.95.

We scrolled down to see what else was offered. There was a Criminal Record Search, an Instant People Locator Search, an Instant First Name Search, an Instant Family Name Search, and—last but not least—for $12.95, a search called Instantly Determine if Someone Is Alive or Deceased.

"Wow," Beamer said. "That might work. It's bound to have the death date, if we can find him."

"Yeah," I agreed. "But how are we going to pay for it? We need a credit card."

Beamer thought for a minute. "I'll ask my grandpa. I'll promise to pay him back. He might not even ask what it's for."

"Go for it," I said.

Beamer got up and went into the living room. About a minute later, he was back with a Visa card.

"What'd he say?" I asked.

"He looked me straight in the eye and said, 'I trust you to use this carefully.' Emphasis on the word *trust*."

"What are they doing?"

"Still reading."

He sat back down and clicked on the last option. A form came up on the screen.

In the space for a name, we typed, "Fine, Irving."

"'State of Death'—what does that mean? What state the body was in?" I asked. "Like 'Decomposed'?"

"No, stupid, what state he died in, like 'Pennsylvania.'"

"Oh," I said. "Sorry. So should we put Pennsylvania, then?"

"Well, he died on his way back from Washington to Pennsylvania. He might have been in Maryland when the wreck happened."

"Yeah, you're right. Maybe we should put 'All states' to be on the safe side. How about 'Approximate Date of Birth'?"

"Oh boy—let's see. If he'd finished college and had a Ph.D. when he died, plus he'd worked at a job for a while, then he must have been in his late twenties at least. Maybe even thirty."

"It says we can do it plus or minus five years. That ought to cover it. So let's say he was twenty-eight. So subtract that from 1953. . . ."

I had to do it on paper, math whiz that I am. It came out that if he was twenty-eight when he died in 1953, he would have been born in 1925.

We entered Mr. Gordon's credit card number and clicked on the send button. Then we sat there, staring at the screen, and waited. After about a minute, the results came up: "Fine, Irving, PA, 12/27/23—2/19/53."

"Yes!" I said. "Now we can find the obituary. It'll be easy! Let's ask your grandma if we can get a ride into Philadelphia with her tomorrow so we can go to the library."

"And what will our reason be?"

"I don't know. To do some research."

"In the middle of the summer?"

"Uh . . . no. I guess not."

We both sat there thinking, not coming up with anything at all.

Mrs. Gordon stuck her head around the door.

"How are you two doing? You looked a little green around the gills when you got home."

"We're fine, Grandma," Beamer said, handing her the credit card. "Could you give that to Grandpa? Tell him thanks. I'll pay him back."

"I wouldn't worry about that, sweetie, unless you charged a Ferrari on it."

"Hey, I didn't think of that. Let me have it back!"

Mrs. Gordon grinned and started to shut the door.

"Oh—Grandma, wait," Beamer said. "Could we go into Philly with you tomorrow?"

"Oh, sweetie, I really can't get away from the office tomorrow, but if you want to see the sights, we could do it next week."

"Well, that would be fun, too, but we want to go to the library. We can hang out there all day. There's lots of stuff to do. You wouldn't have to take off work."

"What—avoiding Marshall, are we?"

Yes! The perfect excuse! I nodded vigorously.

"Well, of course, I'd love that," she said. "But you need to be ready by eight-thirty. Do you have an alarm clock?"

"I do," I said. "We'll be ready."

Mrs. Gordon had just shut the door, when the phone rang. We heard Mr. Gordon pick up in the kitchen.

"This is the Gordon residence," he said.

There was a pause. "Harper's Mill . . . Yes . . . Yes, that would be my grandson, Scott, I would imagine. . . . Yes, Franny, she's our guest. . . . Of course. Just a minute." Then, louder: "Scott! Telephone for you."

Beamer picked up the extension. "Hello?" he said.

I had this weird feeling. When Beamer's eyes went wide and his jaw dropped, I knew.

"How . . . how did you find us?" Beamer stammered.

I leaned over and angled the receiver so I could hear, too. It was a woman's voice. I heard the word *redial*.

Oh, man—of course! One glance at the office would have told her everything, beginning with the telephone still sitting on the floor. It was obvious we had used it. All she had to do was wait till we got home and then press the redial button. And Mr. Gordon had helpfully provided her with his name and the name of the town.

"I believe you have something that belongs to me," Ida May said, her voice hard.

"Y . . . yes," Beamer said softly.

"So tell me," she went on, "just out of curiosity. What made you think you had the right to break into my house and go through my files and steal my belongings?"

"I'm sorry," Beamer said. "It's just . . ."

"Oh, skip it," she said. "I don't really want to know. I'd rather tell you what I'm going to do about it. Wouldn't that be more interesting? See, first, I'm going to tell that very nice grandfather of yours what his sweet little grandson and his adorable little guest were up to this afternoon. I imagine that will disappoint him a great deal, don't you? Then, of course, I will call the police."

"Oh, please don't."

"Please don't? Please don't? Then perhaps you'd like to return my tape. Right now."

"We can't right now," Beamer said, sounding desperate. "It's nighttime. We don't have any way to get there."

"I don't want to see you, you moron. I've seen quite enough of you already. What I want is the tape."

"But how—"

"Listen to me. I want you to put that tape in an envelope. I want you to seal it. I want you to address it to me at One four oh seven Pleasant Hill Road. I want it postmarked before noon tomorrow. Is that clear?"

"Crystal."

"Because if you don't, you are going to be in more trouble than you can possibly imagine. Breaking and entering, burglary—that's pretty serious stuff. And we're really tough on crime these days, you know. You look old enough to be tried as adults. . . ."

"We'll do it," Beamer said. "I promise."

"Good. Now one more thing. You have no more right to watch that tape than you had to take it. Got that?"

"Yes," Beamer said.

"You are *not* to watch that tape."

"Absolutely. We promise."

20

The tape opened with a shot of a green armchair. I recognized it as the one in the living room at Ida's house. The chair was empty, but brightly lighted. After a few seconds, Ida appeared on the screen and sat down in the chair. She must have been filming herself.

She had dressed up for the occasion in a dark dress and pearls. She looked better than when we'd seen her, though the light from the video camera really bleached out her skin. She licked her lips quickly, like a lizard, then began. She talked straight into the camera.

"My name is Ida May Fine," she said. "I am the author of forty children's books, which I wrote under the name I. M. Fine. Thirty-nine of them were part of the Chillers series. Many of you, no doubt, have heard of me. You read my books back in the time before everything changed.

"They sold very well indeed. Once the Chillers series was established, my publisher, Riverbend Press, shipped almost a million copies of my books every month. I really don't know the grand total of copies sold, but it's in the multimillions. And in addition, they were published in twenty different languages. To appreciate the full extent of my readership, you must remember that a great number of those books sold to libraries, where they were read by many, many children."

"What is this?" I said to Beamer. "Some kind of bragfest?"

"Looks like it."

Ida May licked her lips again and adjusted her sitting posture. She glanced down, as though she was thinking what to say next.

"That gave me enormous power," she said, flashing a tight little goody-for-me smile. "As you can imagine. Money, too, of course, though I never cared for money. A lot of people say that, but they rarely mean it. I really do. I wanted the power, though, because I wanted to change the world. And I did. Those of you listening to me now are living with the consequences."

I gasped. This wasn't what I had expected at all.

"My father, Irving Fine, wanted to change the world, in his own small way. He was a gifted scientist and a fine teacher. He must surely have believed that his work would benefit mankind. And he must also have assumed the community would reward him with respect and gratitude.

"But no—that's not what happened. You see, he was accused of selling scientific secrets to the Russians, of betraying his country. Destroyed his reputation, and if he hadn't died in an accident first, they would have put him in prison. Which was really unfortunate because, you see, it turned out to be a terrible mistake. He was completely innocent. Such an easy thing, isn't it, to ruin a man's life?

"No, my father had no desire to harm this country or bring down the government. None whatsoever.

"And you know what? *That was his big mistake.*"

My hair stood on end.

"In the years after his death, I came to realize that the society I was living in was beyond saving. It was corrupt, it was cruel, and it would go on being corrupt and cruel until someone brought it to its knees. It was already stumbling. I decided to give it a little push."

Ida May leaned forward, hands on knees, elbows out, like a spider about to spring.

"Which brings me to the reason I am speaking to you now. I want you to know how things got to be the way they are. I am sure there are lots of pundits out there analyzing and explaining the surprising downfall of modern civilization. Trust me. They don't have a clue what happened.

"It was my last book, *The Avenging Word*, that changed the world you live in. That's rather touching, don't you think? Not a bomb. Not a plague. A children's book!

"It was one of my best. I used every trick I knew to draw my readers in, to make it 'a real page-turner,' as they say. It was positively irresistible—right up to page sixty-eight."

She sat back then, a little smile of satisfaction on her face.

"What happened after page sixty-eight? You remember, surely! There were so many of you, all over America—all over the world. After page sixty-eight, you simply put . . . the . . . book . . . down. It was the last book you ever read, wasn't it? Because after that, you were not *able* to read. Not ever again."

Beamer paused the tape so we could stare at each other. "Do you think she could actually do that?" he asked.

I just shook my head and shrugged. I couldn't find the words. Beamer pressed the play button and Ida's mouth started moving again.

"How? That's what you're wondering. How could she do that? Well, of course I'm not going to tell you. Not the details, anyway. But I will tell you that many years ago, during a brief stint in graduate school, I spent a lot of time in the library reading very dusty old books. You would be amazed what you can find in a university library. I came across an ancient text on mind control. Now, if you had come across that book, you would probably have said it was about 'magic.' I thought so, too, at first. But upon closer inspection, I realized that it was something far more exciting, far more powerful. It was a book on the *science* of magic. Not abracadabra. Not hocus-pocus. *Real* magic.

"I took it from the library," she said. "I have it with me here."

She reached over toward a table that was offscreen and got the book. She placed it lovingly in her lap.

"Would it work? I wondered. Could I insert messages into something I wrote—a letter, say, or a story—that would cause the reader to do anything I wanted him to? I was just curious, you understand. So I tried it. I wrote a note to one of my professors, a very

154

unpleasant and arrogant man, and left it on his desk before class. He came in, glanced at it—and then he started hopping around the room, like a rabbit."

Ida made paws with her hands and grinned.

"I'm sure his reputation never recovered from that incident.

"Anyway, once I knew it worked, I began to think about how I could use such power. I thought about it for years. Eventually, I started writing.

"I knew someone who worked in the children's books department of Riverbend Press. I asked if she would look at a ghost story for children that I had written. She thought it was good. Riverbend published it that year, and it sold quite well for a first book.

"The editor suggested the Chillers series, and I was off and running. I discovered I had a real knack for writing, and . . . well, I already mentioned how successful I became. Then, when my readership had reached a truly phenomenal level, I tried a few practice runs. All of them were successful.

"I knew the time had come to write *The Avenging Word*. As I speak to you now, it is ready for publication. In a few months, it will hit the bookstores, and the world transformation you are living with now . . . will begin. To be more precise, it has already begun, for my editor—

alas!—has had to give up his job. He's working over at Tastee-Freez now. Suddenly, inexplicably, he found himself unable to read a word! The copyeditor has retired, too. I needn't tell you why."

"Cripes, Beamer!" I said.

"It will be fascinating to watch what happens next. The school system will collapse, I have no doubt, pouring massive numbers of young people out into the workforce who can't hold down skilled jobs. Whole sections of our economy will gradually go bankrupt and put people out of work. First, of course, the obvious ones: publishers, magazine companies, bookstores, libraries. And we certainly won't need newspapers anymore. I guess you'll have to get your news on TV.

"I lie awake at night thinking about it. Trying to find one single corner of our economy that will not come tumbling down eventually. And you see, that's the beauty of it all—every sector of our economy depends on some other sector. So it's like those famous dominoes—first one goes, then another. Then they're all down.

"Now, machines are key to the whole collapse, because they make our economy run. But soon we won't have any engineers or technicians. No one to design our automobiles or our computers or our electrical power plants. No one to build them or repair them, either.

"As the years pass—this is my favorite part—the only ones left who will know anything will be the old people. They won't be walking around miserable anymore, wishing they were young, instead of flabby and wrinkled and bald—it will be the *young* people walking around feeling miserable because they don't know how to *do* anything and the *old* people have all the power. Of course, people won't live as long as they do today—not when there aren't any doctors left to do their triple-bypass operations.

"Before long, we'll be back to making soap and candles at home. Now, isn't that something? All of that monumental disaster from one little children's book! More powerful than a *thousand* bombs."

Now she leaned forward again and looked hard into the camera lens—at us. She was getting ready to sum up.

"Did I get it right? Did I describe the world you live in? Are you wondering now just why I would do such a thing? Well, I will tell you. Because maybe now you can all begin to look at one another as fellow human beings. It's hard to be smug when the rug's been pulled out from under you. You know how it feels to suffer. Maybe, after a while, you will build again. A new world. A better world. I won't live to see it, but it is my gift to you. Use it well."

21

The next morning, we asked Mrs. Gordon to swing by the post office on our way to Philadelphia. Here's what I was thinking as we waited in line to mail the pachage: Grown-ups—even really smart grown-ups—don't have a clue how far behind kids they are, technologically speaking. They're just so used to knowing more than we do about pretty much everything. But who do they go to when their computers crash or they can't program their VCRs? They go to us, that's who. And yet they always seem so surprised when some twelve-year-old hacks into the Pentagon's computer network or starts a web business that makes a million dollars. What is my point here? Well, my point is that apparently it hadn't occurred to Ida that we could easily copy that tape. All we'd needed was the Gordons' video camera and a blank tape.

Whether we could take it to the police or not, it was still crucial evidence. For one thing, it would make it a lot easier to convince Ida's family—or any other adult, for that matter—that our outlandish story wasn't just the product of overactive imaginations. Now, armed with the above-mentioned evidence, our next step was to find the above-mentioned family.

Mrs. Gordon dropped us off at the Free Library of Philadelphia right at 9:00. This made her a little late for work, but she didn't want to get us there before it opened. She made us promise to stay in the library and not to go wandering around. She said she'd come by at lunchtime and take us to a nice little sandwich shop she knew. She watched to make sure we got inside safely. Then we were on our own.

We found the newspaper section and asked the librarian there how we would go about finding an obituary from 1953. He walked us over to some shelves filled with boxes of microfilm, each marked with the dates and the names of the newspapers. Then he showed us how to thread the microfilm onto the machine.

Pages whizzed by as we turned the handle. It was really fascinating seeing those old pictures and corny ads. For a second, I was tempted to stop and read some of them. But then I reminded myself why we were there and kept turning.

We had started with the *Philadelphia Inquirer* and were looking for February 20, 1953, the day after Irving died. If we didn't find it there, we'd check February 21. The librarian said it sometimes took a day or two for an obit to get into the paper.

At last, we found the front page for February 21, then scrolled down carefully, page by page, looking for the obituaries.

"There it is!" Beamer whispered, pointing to a headline that was just rising up from the bottom of the screen:

ACCUSED SCIENTIST, WIFE KILLED IN CRASH

I rolled it up and centered it on the screen:

University of Pennsylvania physics professor Irving Fine, who was returning home after testifying before the House Committee on Un-American Activities, was killed last evening when his car skidded off the road in a snowstorm. His wife, Ruth, was also killed.

"Oh, man!" Beamer whispered. "They were both killed!"

"Yeah," I whispered back. "That's horrible!"

Fine was born in Wimberly, Pennsylvania, and received a bachelor's degree in physics from Columbia University and a Ph.D. from Princeton. He married the former Ruth Cohen of Brooklyn and taught at the University of Pennsylvania, becoming the youngest professor in that university's history to gain full tenure. He was noted not only for his innovative research but also for his dynamic teaching skills. His Physics for Poets was among the most popular courses offered at the university.

His career came to a dramatic halt when it was alleged that sensitive material from his lab had been discovered in the possession of a Russian espionage agent. Dr. Fine was involved in an important project for the government, the details of which were not made available to the public, except that it was related to weapons research.

In his testimony, Fine denied any involvement in espionage and admitted only that security at his lab was lax.

Fine is survived by twin daughters, Iris and Ida, and a sister, Mildred Calloway, all of Wimberly.

"Twin daughters!" I gasped. "That means there are *two* of them out there. What a scary thought."

"Maybe," Beamer said. "Maybe not. The other one

might be normal. In which case, that's a good thing. I mean, we're looking for family—somebody who might make her stop. And what could be closer than a twin sister?"

"Yeah," I agreed. "If we can find her. Come on, let's put this stuff away."

So we returned the microfilm to its proper place and headed for the library's computers. By now, we were old pros at the "find a person" sites. In no time, we had located several people named Iris Fine, complete with phone numbers and addresses. One in Council Bluffs, Iowa. One in Richmond, Virginia. And one in Tyler, Texas.

I wasn't holding out a lot of hope, though, because I thought it was pretty likely that our Iris had long since married and changed her name. Plus, there was a good chance that since it was the middle of the morning, they would all be at work. We'd probably just get answering machines. But we had their phone numbers and the rest of the day to kill, so we got a whole lot of quarters from the change machine next to the copier and headed for the pay phone.

The Iowa Iris was at home and sounded about eighty. She had never lived in Pennsylvania and didn't have a twin sister. She was really sweet, though, and said she sure hoped we found the right one.

The Virginia Iris wasn't there. The woman who answered the phone said she was the housekeeper. Mrs. Fine was at the beauty shop. "Would you like to call back later?" she asked.

"*Mrs.* Fine," I said. "So Fine is her married name?"

"Yes," the housekeeper said. "Mr. Fine passed on about ten years ago."

The Texas Iris wasn't there, either. Just a young-sounding voice with a thick drawl saying, "Hi. I'm not here. Leave a message." I hung up. We could call her back later, but I knew there really wasn't any point. She sounded way too young to be Ida's twin and way too southern to have grown up in Pennsylvania.

"Now what?" I said.

Beamer was sitting on the floor by the pay phone, leaning against the wall, his face in his hands. He let out a huge sigh.

"Come on, Beamer. Help me out here."

"Call the candy guy," he said.

"Jake Bermann?"

"Yeah. She put his Jelly Worms in her book. Then she named her dog Jake."

"You're right. She did!"

"And he lived in Wimberly when the Fine twins

were growing up. He must have known them. Maybe he can tell us something about Iris. Like if she married a local guy, he might know her married name."

So Beamer called Kute Kandy and asked for Edna Franklin, who gave him Mr. Bermann's telephone number in Florida. She said she didn't usually give his number out to people, but we seemed like such nice kids. She just hoped we would keep in mind that he was quite elderly and not say anything to upset him. Beamer thanked her and hung up.

We went back to the change machine for more quarters. Then I dialed the number.

22

ello." It was a man's voice. He had a thick accent. German, maybe.

"Is this Mr. Jake Bermann?" I asked, holding the receiver at an angle so Beamer could hear.

"Yes. Who is this, please?"

"Um, my name is Franny Sharp. Mrs. Franklin— from Kute Kandy?—well, she said it was all right if I called you."

"She did? Well, sure. That's fine. What can I do for you?"

"Okay, well we—I—need some help finding someone. Maybe you knew her in Wimberly a long time ago."

"Could be. Who, exactly?"

"Well, actually, it's two people. Iris and Ida Fine. They were twins. Their father was named Irving Fine and he was killed in a car wreck in 1953."

"Oh, yes," he said. "I remember that. Such a sad thing. The wife was killed also."

My heart leapt with excitement. He remembered them!

"And the two little girls," I said. "They lived with their aunt, Mrs. Calloway? Is that right? Lived up on Pleasant Hill Road?"

He made a sort of noise in his throat like he was about to spit, only I think it was just his way of showing how disgusted he was. "No," he said. "That Mrs. Calloway did not raise those children. That Mrs. Calloway put them both in the orphan home, if you can believe that."

"No kidding?"

"No kidding."

"Where was that? The orphan home?"

"In Wimberly—it's gone now. It wasn't such a bad place, you understand. But such a shame for those little girls. And shame on Mrs. Calloway is what I think."

"Gosh, that's weird," I said. "I wonder why. I mean, I've seen that house she lived in. It's plenty big."

"Oh, she was ashamed of her brother, Irving. He was in trouble—bad trouble—and she didn't want any of it to rub off on her. She had a rich husband and the big house. She just wanted to live like a rich lady, I guess."

"Did you know the little girls? Did you see them around town or anything?"

He laughed. "I had a candy shop," he said. "I saw all the kids."

"What can you tell us about them? Anything at all."

"Well, let me think. Pretty little redheaded girls, such curly, curly hair."

"Were they identical twins? You know, did they look the same?"

"Oh, yes, identical. Dressed alike and always together, always holding hands. Never saw the one without the other. Then after the parents died, like I said, they went to the orphan home. But they still came by the store after school two, three times a week. Then one day, there was just the one of them.

"So I says, 'Which one are you?' and she says, 'I'm Ida'—kind of whimpering, you know. So I says, 'Where's your sister?' and she says, 'Adopted.'

"Well, I couldn't believe it, you see. 'Just her? Not you?' I asked. And she shook her head. so sad, and just cried her little heart out."

"Iris was *adopted*?"

"Yes. Like I said, I just couldn't believe it. So I went over there, to the orphan home, and asked the director, 'Couldn't you keep those two babies together?' and he said he had tried real hard, but nobody wanted two. It was hard enough to find homes for them, he said, as old as they were."

"Did . . . did she live there in the . . . in Wimberly? With her new family?"

"No. The people were from Philadelphia. But Ida said they were moving anyway. California, I think."

"Iris would have a different name, then, wouldn't she? After she got adopted?"

"Yes. But I don't know what it was. She just disappeared."

"Wow!" I said. "What happened after that?"

"To Ida? She grew up. Moved away. She was smart, you know. Went to college."

"Did she have friends? Did she get over being sad about her mom and dad and sister?" The minute I asked that question, I wondered whether *anybody* could get over losing a whole family like that.

"Excuse me," Mr. Bermann said. "But I wonder— why are you asking about Ida? Did something happen to her?"

"No," I said. "Not exactly. It's sort of complicated. She's kind of mad at the world, actually."

"Mad at the world, huh? She had a right to be mad, I think. There were a lot of not-so-nice kids, you know. Treated her real bad. Talked to her mean about her father. Put gum in her hair once, so she had to cut out this big chunk of it. And then they called her 'Baldy.' I wouldn't let those kids in my store. So they broke the window one night. Wrote things on my door. It was mostly just these three or four boys, but lots of others went along. You know how that is. Scared of 'em, I guess."

"Mr. Bermann, did you know that Ida is a writer now?"

"I was pretty sure that was Ida—the I. M. Fine who writes those kids' books. She wrote about Jelly Worms in her book, and all of a sudden we couldn't fill all the orders. I wondered, you know. Thought it had to be her. Doing me a little favor after all these years."

"She didn't call or write or anything, after she moved back?"

"She moved back? To Wimberly?"

"Yeah. She lives up in Mrs. Calloway's old house. That's why we thought, you know, that she had grown up there."

"Well, well," he said. "Imagine that. Ida got to live in that house after all. I guess the old lady didn't have anybody else to leave it to."

I was running out of quarters.

"Mr. Bermann, I have to go now, but thank you so much for helping us. And . . . I may need to call back. Would that be okay?"

"Yes, of course. I'm not going anywhere."

We hung up.

Beamer and I both sat down on the library floor. Neither of us said anything for a while. We were each thinking our own thoughts.

"We'll never find Iris," I said finally. "She's had a different last name since she was a kid. She moved away. The orphan home is out of business."

"You're probably right," Beamer said. "I guess our only hope is to get Jake to call Ida. He seemed really nice, and we know she likes him. We'd have to send him the tape, though. 'Cause otherwise he'd never believe us."

"Yeah, I agree. But I don't think a phone call is going to do it. I think he's going to have to go there in person."

"It'll cost a lot—flying up here from Florida."

"Yeah, but he's rich. I bet he'd pay his own way."

"What if he's too old to travel?"

"I didn't think of that. He might be."

We were both quiet for a while.

"Man, she really got gypped," I said finally. "You know that? Iris gets the new family and Ida gets the orphan home and the Wimberly bullies."

"Yup," he agreed.

"I wonder what she's like—Iris. I mean, think of it—she's an exact copy of Ida, only she's lived a totally different life!"

"Yeah, that is weird to think about. That there could be another, identical . . ."

"What?"

Beamer just sat there like a dog who'd heard a noise and was about to bark bloody murder.

"*What?*"

He put his face in his hands. Then he looked up.

"I just . . . had a thought."

"Well, congratulations!"

He glared at me out of the corner of his eyes but didn't say anything.

"Beamer!"

"Wait. Hold on. Give me some time."

"Time for what?"

"To figure something out. I just have a hunch. Let's hold off on Mr. Bermann till I check it out. I promise I'll tell you if I'm wrong. But it will be *so* cool if I'm right."

That night, he went into the study, shut the door, and made a long phone call. I sat out in the living room, alternately excited because he apparently had a lead and steaming mad because he wouldn't tell me what it was. Beamer can be so exasperating. I mean, whose brainstorm was this whole I. M. Fine thing, anyway?

When he came out, he was smiling like he'd just won the Nobel Prize or something.

"I hate it when you're smug," I said.

Beamer just kept on smiling.

"Trust me," he said. "It'll be a lot more fun this way."

The next morning, Beamer decided we should make pancakes. It was perfectly clear to me that he was just killing time, waiting for something to happen. But hey—might as well have a nice breakfast while you're waiting to be amazed.

So we got out Mrs. Gordon's *Fannie Farmer Cookbook* and found a recipe for pancakes. Beamer said his dad likes to add fresh blueberries to the batter, only there weren't any in the refrigerator. He thought canned pineapple might make a good substitute, but I nixed that idea. There wasn't any syrup in the house, either, so we just made do with powdered sugar. Still, all in all, our pancakes were pretty good—if you didn't count the first batch.

It was a pretty complex operation, what with looking for ingredients and breaking eggs and measuring flour and milk and figuring out that if you set the burner on high, your pancakes got burned. And then there was eating them—which, naturally, was the best part—followed by the wiping off of counters and putting all the stuff in the dishwasher. It took the better part of an hour. And the whole time, I kept catching Beamer glancing at the clock.

What the heck was going to happen?

Shortly before noon, we heard a car pull into the drive. Beamer lit up like Times Square and dashed to the kitchen window. I was after him so fast, I practically knocked him into the sink. Peering over his shoulder, I saw a white Toyota and, inside, a flash of red hair.

"Beamer?" I said, astonished, leaning closer to make sure. *"Mrs. Lamb?"*

"Y . . . e . . . s," he said, dragging the word out slowly. Obviously, there was something else—the *big* something—which I was supposed to figure out.

The car door opened and Mrs. Lamb got out, brushed her skirt smooth, and looked around at the jungle of trees that surround the Gordons' house. As she stood there in the driveway, the sun lit up her hair and—

"Beamer!"

23

It's Iris! Mrs. Lamb is Iris!"

Beamer just grinned.

"How did you know? Oh, Beamer—you're such a genius! They look so different! Ida is so skinny and sour and her hair is all short. . . ."

Beamer kept smiling. "When we were watching that tape, the whole time I kept thinking I knew her somehow, you know? But obviously, I didn't. I thought maybe it was just some famous person she reminded me of, only I couldn't think of who."

"Me, too. For a second anyway. But then it got all creepy and I never gave it another thought."

"And there was something about her voice, too. You know, kind of deep and strong. It reminded me of Mrs. Lamb's."

"So when did you put it all together?"

"It was when we were talking yesterday, after we called Jake. You know—that there was this *exact copy* of Ida walking around out there somewhere? And, well, she's so unusual-looking, with that red hair and the pale skin and the blue eyes. And I was trying to picture someone who looked like that, only, you know, normal. And then it just clicked."

Mrs. Lamb passed near the kitchen window on her way to the front door. If she had turned her head, she would have seen us looking at her. There was an anxious expression on her face, like a kid on the way to the principal's office. Which wasn't surprising, I guess—she was about to see her twin sister for the first time in almost fifty years!

Beamer slipped the copied tape into the VCR. He turned to look at Mrs. Lamb, a little nervously, I thought.

"Ready?" he said.

She made a sort of helpless gesture with her hands. She clearly didn't know how to feel about the whole thing. "Play it," she said. "Let's see what you've got."

When the tape began and Ida was seated in her chair, talking, Mrs. Lamb asked Beamer to pause it. She went up closer to the TV and studied the face. I was watching her back and I could see her take a sudden big breath. "Yes," she said. Then she came back and sat down. "All right, go ahead."

I tried not to stare at Mrs. Lamb while she was watching the tape, but I couldn't help it. First of all, I wanted to see whether she was going to believe it or not. But also, I just couldn't imagine how a person would react to such a thing: finding your long-lost twin sister—and then hearing that same twin sister admit she was out to destroy the world. I mean, that's pretty heavy stuff.

Well, in case you're curious, she started out looking a little wary. Then when Ida got to the part about her father, Mrs. Lamb started to cry. I ran to the bathroom to get her some Kleenex. Toward the end of the tape, I stopped looking at Mrs. Lamb at all. She seemed so stricken, it didn't seem right for me to watch.

The drive to Wimberly took us half the time it took to go by bus.

"Did you bring the pictures?" Beamer asked.

Mrs. Lamb patted her purse, beside her there on the seat. "Right here," she said.

"What pictures?" I asked.

"All kinds," Mrs. Lamb said. "Pictures of me when I was little. Pictures of my husband and my kids. Pictures of my grandkids."

"Wow," I said. "A whole family she doesn't know."

Mrs. Lamb just shook her head in silent agreement. Tears were welling up in her eyes again.

"Do you really think you can win her over?" I asked.

"I truly hope so," she said, and fished a Kleenex out of her purse.

We parked in front of the house. Mrs. Lamb just sat there in the car for a while, staring up at it.

"I don't remember this place," she said finally. "You say it was my aunt's house?"

"Mildred Calloway," I said. "Your father's sister. Maybe you never even came here. She wouldn't take you in after your parents died. That's what Mr. Bermann said. Because of your dad—well, the spy thing and all."

"I sort of remember that," Mrs. Lamb said. "More a shadow of a feeling, really. I couldn't have described it or quoted actual words. But there was this blue carpet with a fancy design. I remember staring at it and feeling just overwhelmed with . . . shame. Like I had done something disgraceful. That's appalling, isn't it? I mean, we were just babies."

Then she pulled herself together. "All right, boys and girls," she said, "are we ready?"

We said we were, and the three of us traipsed up the hill.

The paint on the porch was still peeling. Solicitors were still not welcome. Beamer rang the bell.

A face appeared in the parlor window, looking out at us. This was the moment I had been waiting for, and it happened just as I knew it would: First, she recognized us, and her face took on this angry scowl. Then, two beats later, the face was still staring, but confusion was washing over it. That woman standing beside us on the porch with masses of unruly red hair, that sweet round face and blue eyes—it was her own face, only happy, not eaten away by bitterness and rage. Then a look that I can only describe as heartbreaking, when she finally understood. The figure in the window raised her hand to the glass, as if to touch her sister's face.

All this took place in a matter of seconds and I was the only one who saw it. Beamer and Mrs. Lamb were watching the door, wondering whether to ring again.

"She's coming," I said. And seconds later, we heard the rustle and click of someone frantically undoing bolt and chain; then the door swung wide open.

The two women stared at each other, afraid to speak.

"*Iris?*" This in a trembling whisper.

"Can you believe it?" Mrs. Lamb said, and took her sister into her arms.

"I searched for you," Ida said between sobs. "For years."

Mrs. Lamb stroked her sister's hair. We knew what she was thinking, because she had told us in the car. With flushed cheeks and her hand on her heart, Mrs. Lamb had admitted that she had never even thought of searching for Ida. She had gradually forgotten Wimberly and the family tragedy. She had started a new life with new parents, who were good to her. Her name wasn't Fine anymore; it was Carter. She moved to California and made friends and started school. And as she got older, those days and those people faded in her memory, until she could scarcely remember them at all. "Isn't that awful?" she had said. "I was so content with my life that I never looked back."

So, anyway, that's why I knew what Mrs. Lamb was feeling, why her voice trembled when she said, "I always dreamed I'd find you one day." She was lying and she felt terrible about it.

When they had finished hugging, Ida remembered us. "Those kids . . ." she began.

"They're my students, Ida. And they're the ones who brought us together."

She glared at us for a few more seconds, then threw up her hands and hugged Mrs. Lamb again. Mrs. Lamb winked at us. Then we all went inside.

It was really weird to be invited, however reluctantly, into a house you had just burgled two days before. There we were, in the very same living room. And there was the same green chair Ida had sat in to record her dying message. Only she didn't sit there that day. She sat on the couch so she and her sister could hold on to each other.

Beamer pulled me back into the entryway.

"I think we should go," he said. "Let them talk alone."

"Yeah, you're right," I said. "But how are we going to get home? Wait across the street till Mrs. Lamb comes out?"

"No, dummy. We'll take the bus. She'll probably spend the night here, anyway. She brought a bag."

He waved at Mrs. Lamb and made a telephone gesture. She nodded. She'd call and let us know how it all turned out.

"Fifty years!" Iris was saying as we left. "Imagine!"

We were feeling pretty proud of ourselves just then, though it was hard to take in the enormity of it all. I mean, we had actually changed the course of history. How do you get your head around that?

"You think Mrs. Lamb can really do it?" I asked.

"Yup," said Beamer, "I do."

"I sure hope you're right."

"Franny?"

"What?"

"We can't tell people about this, you know."

"Couldn't we just leave out the part about breaking and entering?"

"It's not just that. It's Ida."

Then I understood. "It would mess her up big-time, wouldn't it?" I said.

"Big-time," he agreed.

We didn't say anything for a while.

"But we know what we did," I pointed out.

"Yeah."

"And someday we can tell our grandchildren," I added.

"Is that a proposal?"

"What?"

"Well, if we're going to have grandchildren, we'll have to get married first."

I punched him.

"Is that a 'No'?"

"Beamer . . ."

"What?"

"Shut up!"

"Okay."

He had a big grin on his face. So did I. We were on top of the world.

24

That night, we had Thai food for dinner. I had never tasted it before, so it was sort of a revelation. There was this grilled meat you dip in peanut sauce. And two different kinds of curries that were kind of spicy and kind of sweet. I know it sounds gross, but it really was fabulous. I told Beamer I would reconsider his proposal if he promised we would live in Thailand.

His grandparents asked more than once why we were in such a silly mood. Was it that field trip we went on with our teacher? And where had we gone, anyway?

"To visit her sister in Wimberly," we said. "She's a writer."

That seemed to satisfy them.

After dinner, we got out the Trivial Pursuit game.

We played boys against the girls, which gave us an advantage, since Mrs. Gordon has one of those steel-trap minds for history and geography and I am good on literature. I admit, we were pretty hopeless on Arts and Entertainment (I mean, who knows the names of people in old seventies sitcoms?) and a little weak on Sports and Leisure (how many points for a bull's-eye in darts?). But still, even with Mr. Gordon being great on science and nature and Beamer pretty fair on sports, the girls definitely ruled that night.

I think our mood was kind of contagious, because Beamer's grandparents got kind of silly, too. We had this huge argument—the kind where nobody is really mad—about whether we should get credit for "Martin Luther King" as an answer when, technically, the person we were referring to was Martin Luther King, *Jr.* Martin Luther King was a whole other person, the father of the civil rights leader.

"So you want to play hardball?" said Mrs. Gordon.

"They're two different people," Beamer insisted. "I can't help it if you got it wrong."

"Okay," she said. "But don't forget. What goes around comes around."

"We can take it," said Mr. Gordon.

"We'll see," said his wife.

That's when the phone rang. Beamer shot out of his chair like he'd just sat on the cat.

His grandparents looked puzzled.

"You want to get that?"

"Yeah," Beamer said, dashing into the study. "It's probably for me."

Ten seconds later, Beamer was back, a disappointed look on his face.

"It's for you," he said. "It's Zoë."

"Zoë?"

"Your sister."

"I know who Zoë is, Beamer," I snapped, and went in to the study to pick up the phone.

"Hi," I said. "What's up?" I couldn't imagine why she would be calling me long-distance.

"We're moving again," she said.

"Oh, great," I moaned. "That is just great."

"But wait, there's more."

"We're moving to Iceland?"

"No, listen," Zoë said. "J.D. overheard Mom and Dad talking last night. Dad was saying he had been offered this job in Cleveland. . . ."

"Wonderful! We've never lived in Ohio. Maybe at this rate, we can make all fifty states before I go off to college."

"Will you shut up and listen? I haven't gotten to the important part. So Dad says that the job would be a lot more challenging and pay more than the *offer to stay on in Baltimore!*"

"Say again?"

"They asked him to stay on as president of the college here."

"No kidding!"

"So, anyway, Mom says, you know, 'It's up to you, sweet face, whatever you want. I can take my work with me.'"

"And?"

"So J.D. comes into my room and tells me all this and then I freak out and all, and he just sits there like he does, looking weird. Then he says, 'They can go to Cleveland if they want to. I'm staying here.'"

I literally had to catch my breath.

"Oh my gosh!" I said. "J.D. is a genius."

"No, he's just weird. But when he said that, you know, I just suddenly realized that if all three of us—"

"Went on strike?"

"Yeah, like that."

"Oh, that is so cool!"

"Are you with us?"

"Yes, of course!"

"Wait—here's J.D."

He came on the line. "Hi," he said.

"Hi back," I said. "I just want you to know that I think you're brilliant."

"Whatever," he said. "I'm just not moving again."

"Have you said anything to them yet?"

"No. Zoë thought we ought to wait and get you in on it."

"Yeah," I agreed. "But I think we need to move fast. If we wait too long, he may turn the Baltimore job down, and then we'll *have* to move. Talk to them tonight. Call me if you need to and I'll back you up."

"They've gone out tonight," he said. "We'll do it tomorrow."

I realized that Beamer was standing in the doorway, watching me curiously. I raised my eyebrows to signal that it was an interesting conversation.

"Okay," I said. "Call me!"

"Wait," said J.D. "Did you ever find I. M. Fine?"

"Oh, sorry, J.D. Yeah, we did. I guess I should have called to tell you—seeing as how you were the one who found out about Wimberly."

"So, what's he like?"

"Well, first off, he's a woman."

"No way!"

"Yes way. Ida May Fine. And she's crazy and out to destroy civilization, only we discovered that our teacher is her long-lost twin sister, and she's over there right now, trying to convince her to stop being evil."

"Wow," said J.D.

"Anyway, it's a long story. I'll tell you every little detail when I get home, only I don't want to tie up the phone. We're waiting to hear whether we saved civilization or not."

"Oh. That's a good line. I think I'll use it next time someone calls selling aluminum siding."

"Good-bye, J.D."

"Good-bye, Franny."

I hung up.

"Well?" said Beamer.

"Zoë and J.D. and I are on strike," I said.

"What do you mean, 'on strike'?" he asked, following me back into the living room.

"My dad got offered a new job in Cleveland."

"Wasn't that destroyed by Jelly Worms?"

"Beamer, this is important! Don't you care whether I move away or not?"

"Yeah, of course I do. I was just being silly."

"Well, pay attention. It turns out he has a choice this time, because he's also got a job offer in Baltimore. It doesn't pay as much, but it would mean we could actually live somewhere—you know, permanently."

"So, what did he decide?" asked Mrs. Gordon, who had been following all this with great interest.

"He hasn't decided anything yet. But *we* have—my brother and sister and I. They can move to Cleveland if they want to, but *we're* staying in Baltimore. Like I said, we're on strike."

"Wow," said Beamer. "Will that work?"

"Well, they're pretty fond of us. I think they'd miss us a lot up there in Cleveland by themselves."

Beamer's grandparents burst out laughing.

"Even *I* will miss you, and you haven't even been here a week!" Mrs. Gordon said.

"Could I join the strike, too?" Beamer asked. "I could make a sign and picket your house. MOVING TO CLEVELAND UNFAIR TO CHILDREN!"

"That's very good, Beamer. I think we *should* have signs. March around in the front yard. Call the TV stations. News vans parked up and down the street."

Just then, the phone rang again. Beamer leapt to his feet and dashed into the study to answer it. His grandparents shot conspiratorial glances at each other and grinned. We were more entertaining than a three-ring circus.

"Hello?"

There was a long pause. All three of us sat there eavesdropping shamelessly.

"*Yes!*" he said triumphantly.

I found myself positively bouncing in my chair.

"Oh, that is so great!" he said.

Another long pause.

"Yeah, hold on. I'll get her."

He ducked into the living room and motioned for me to come into the study.

Giving me a thumbs-up, he handed me the phone.

"Hello . . . Franny?" It was Mrs. Lamb.

"Hi, Mrs. Lamb," I said. "Did it go okay?"

"Yes, sweetheart. It did. Ida called the publishers this afternoon and they agreed to let her make some minor revisions . . . to page sixty-eight."

"That's great," I said. "That is so great!"

"You know, I don't think I've properly thanked the two of you. For helping me find my sister, for stopping her from making such an awful mistake. I will be forever grateful, Franny."

"No problem," I said.

"I'll be staying on here for a few more days," Mrs. Lamb said. "Then Ida and I will drive back to Baltimore together."

"Will you stop by here on the way?"

"No, Franny, I don't think so. But I'll see you in the fall."

"Yeah, okay," I said. "Bye, then." And I hung up.

When we went back into the living room, Beamer's grandparents were out of their minds with curiosity.

"What was that all about?" Mrs. Gordon asked.

Beamer grinned. "Oh, nothing much," he said. "Your turn. Roll the dice."

25

H. L. Mencken Middle School is brand-new. The air smells of paint and just-laid carpets. The bulletin boards are empty. The floor is spotless. There are no trophies in the trophy cases and no dents or scrapes on the hallway walls. There aren't even any books on the library shelves. But they're coming, I've been told.

For me, it's another new beginning—but then, I ought to be used to that by now. I've spent my entire life learning peoples' names and struggling to remember whether the lunchroom is down the hall on the right or around the corner on the left. Only this time, it's even more confusing, because in middle school you go to a different room and have a different teacher for each and every subject. Plus, the place is five times as big as Park Place Intermediate.

But for once, I'm not alone in feeling lost and out of place. At Mencken, everybody is starting over, even the eighth graders!

We're a lot of little fish in a great big pond now, and the people who were stars in their old schools are just nameless faces in the crowd. DeeDee, for instance. She showed up on the first day of school ready to knock 'em dead, looking about seventeen and gorgeous with her short skirt and carefully applied makeup. And then she looked around and realized that, for the first time in her life, she had serious competition. There were lots of pretty girls—Valerie, Jennifer, Claudia, Lauren— and each one was the former uncontested glamour queen of her old school. Most of them are really nice to everybody, so they made friends right away. DeeDee started in with her smart remarks and got labeled as a snob. She caught on, though—I'll give her that. Now she's so sweet, it's disgusting. We'll see if it lasts.

On the other hand, the people who were not necessarily stars in their old schools, regular kids like Beamer and me, get a fresh start. The cliques aren't set; the leaders aren't chosen. It's nice to have an even playing field for once.

As you have no doubt gathered, we're still in Baltimore.

Zoë and her friends made masses of protest signs (my favorite? MOVING MADNESS MUDDLES MUNCH-KINS!) and had them out in the yard and all over the house when Dad got home. So he walked through the door, and there were J.D. and Zoë, holding their signs and chanting, "Hey! Hey! Ho! Ho! We've decided not to go!" Then, while he stood there with his jaw hanging open, they started marching around the couch and chairs, chanting, "Unfair! Unfair!" until Dad screamed for them to stop.

Ah, how I wish I'd been there! He was flabbergasted. He'd never realized—got that?—that it bothered us so much to move every year! And this is a man with a *Ph.D.*

So instead of spending the summer watching our household belongings disappear into cardboard boxes, which would then be loaded into a great big truck that would block the street and annoy the neighbors—though that wouldn't really matter because, hey, you'd never see them again!—as I said, instead of doing that, I hung out with Beamer all summer. We put on an Alfred Hitchcock Film Festival for Zoë and J.D., complete with popcorn. We taught a couple of Beamer's dogs to heel (not as easy as you might think). I read him *The Bronze Bow* and *My Brother Sam Is Dead* while he worked on his construction. We got lessons on how to make wontons from Beamer's dad. All in all, my best summer ever.

Then August arrived and we started school. This, as I've already mentioned, was something of an adventure, and I was too busy running to my locker to get my science book and trying to find room Q210 and stuff like that to think about anything else. Or almost too busy, anyway. Distracting as it all was, I could never quite forget that the publication date for *The Avenging Word*—posted on the Riverbend Press website—was September 15. And even though I knew that Ida May had taken out the bad part—well, I just couldn't rest easy until the book was out there and kids were reading it and I could see for myself that no harm had been done.

So we waited. And when September 15 arrived— sure enough, copies of *The Avenging Word* showed up in abundance, clutched in the sweaty hands of half the population of H. L. Mencken Middle School. Kids were reading it on the bus and in line at the lunchroom. Some were even reading it in class. As far as we could tell, none of them suddenly lost the ability to read. I even questioned a couple of kids. You know—"So, is that a good book?"—that kind of thing. And some of them said it was just the most exciting, fabulous book they had ever opened, but others said it got off to a great start and then kind of lost steam and they weren't going to finish it. I guess Ida hadn't put all that much work into the book past page sixty-eight.

There was one other thing we noticed. Usually, there is a kind of pattern to the I. M. Fine phenomenon. A few fanatics get the book the very first day it's out. Then there is a sort of groundswell of interest, until it seems like everybody in America between the ages of seven and fifteen is reading it. Then a gradual tapering off. Like with the Jelly Worm fad. It usually lasted about two months. Only this time, it was pretty much over after two weeks.

Not that it really matters. The important thing is that nobody was harmed. And you have Beamer and me to thank for that.

One day in late September, we went over to Park Place after school to see Mrs. Lamb. We remembered that she usually stayed late on Thursdays, so that's when we went.

"Franny and Scott!" she said when we came into the room. "I've been meaning to call you!"

She scooted a couple of desks up next to hers, then sat down and gazed at us, her chin cradled in her hands.

She was grinning like she'd just won the lottery and we were there to deliver the money.

"So how did it all turn out?" I asked. "We're dying to know."

"Well . . ." Mrs. Lamb said. "Ida's been here in Baltimore all summer. It's been pretty amazing, introducing her to all this family she'd never met—my children, my grandchildren. We spend a lot of time telling stories, catching up. Both of us have blanks to fill in, you know."

"So, is she happier now?"

"Yes, I think she is. She's laid some things to rest that were . . . oh, I don't know—holding her back. Making her angry. It's an important step."

"That's good," I said. "Is she still mad at us?"

"Well, she's upset about the way you invaded her privacy."

We both nodded, embarrassed.

"But I guess she's not too mad. She said for me to tell you she was sending a little gift. Something you would particularly appreciate."

"Really?" I said, not sure whether I liked the sound of that or not.

Mrs. Lamb could see that I was worried. and she reached over to squeeze my hand. "She promised me it was a nice gift. That you would like it."

"Do you know what it is?"

"No. She just said to tell you that you would *know* when it arrived."

"But Mrs. Lamb," Beamer said, "are you sure she's not—you know—trying to get back at us? Sending us a stink bomb, or something worse?"

"No, Scott, please don't worry. She asked me all about you. She was curious, you know—and impressed that you were the only ones who caught on to what she was up to. I told her what smart kids you are—how you did a sixth-grade book report on *David Copperfield*. That really blew her away."

"Really?"

"Yup—she said that if you liked *David Copperfield*, then you must be okay. She has a real thing for Dickens— all those story lines about abused and abandoned children. She really identified with that, I guess."

"Do you think she's going to write any more books?"

"Not *that* kind of book, anyway. She canceled her remaining contracts for the Chillers series, so that's all over now."

"But will she write anything else? Other than Chillers, I mean?"

"Well, she hasn't said, exactly, and I try not to pry

too much. But I can assure you that if she ever does get an itch to write again, she won't add any . . . well, special effects, if you know what I mean."

"No more magic?"

"No more magic. She's put all that behind her. All she talks about now is finding a house in the country with a bit of land." Mrs. Lamb kind of chuckled. "She wants to raise horses. And maybe get some more dogs."

"How's Jake?" Beamer asked.

"Oh, he's such a sweet dog. We've really grown very attached to him."

"Me, too," Beamer said.

I noticed a couple of framed pictures sitting on her desk. They hadn't been there the year before. I peered around to take a look.

One of them was a head-and-shoulders snapshot of Ida, with trees in the background. Her hair had grown out some. She was smiling.

"Nice picture," I said. "She looks more like you now."

Mrs. Lamb nodded. "Yes," she said, "I think so, too."

Then I checked out the other picture. It was old, in black and white, taken in a photographer's studio. It showed a painfully thin, angular, dark-haired man with cheekbones like a Cherokee and beautiful dark eyes. He stood with his arm around a very young woman with wild, curly hair.

"Is that . . ."

"My parents," Mrs. Lamb said. "We found the pictures when we were cleaning out the old house. I guess Aunt Mildred couldn't quite bring herself to throw them away."

"They look so young," Beamer said.

"They were. I think this must have been their engagement picture. They were just out of college then."

"Did you find any baby pictures?"

"A few."

"Wow," I said. "It's like you got your past back."

"Yes, Franny, that's exactly what it's like. Both of us got our past back."

She just looked at us for a minute, with her head tilted a little and a thoughtful smile on her face. Then she got to her feet.

"I hate this, you two, but I really have to go. Promise you'll come back soon?"

"Sure," we said, following her out of the room and down the hall.

"Do you need a ride home?" she asked.

"No thanks. We have our bikes."

"Bye, then, you two. Don't be strangers."

A couple of weeks later, Beamer and I went to the library. (I think I mentioned before that our school library is currently without books, which makes it pretty useless except as a place to do your homework during lunch period.)

Anyway, I was sitting at the big library table, trying to decide whether to check out *The Adventures of Tom Sawyer* or *Twenty Thousand Leagues Under the Sea*, when our friend the librarian came over to chat.

"Franny and Beamer, right?" she said.

"You have a very good memory," I told her.

"Not really. I just remember the interesting people."

"Are we interesting?"

"Definitely. *Tom Sawyer*, huh? Good book. Have you given up on I. M. Fine?"

"Yeah. That's all over now."

"Yes. So it seems," she said.

"What do you mean," Beamer asked, "'So it seems?'"

"Well, it's really very odd. Those books used to be so popular with the kids. And then all of a sudden, no one is reading them at all! And that newest one? *The Avenging Word*? I swear, not a single kid has finished that book. They get about halfway through and then they bring it back and say it was really boring. I mean, it must be *really* bad. I'm tempted to read it myself, just out of curiosity. But I can tell you—it has completely turned the kids off the whole series."

"Good," I said.

I decided on *Tom Sawyer*—I'd read *Twenty Thousand Leagues* next, maybe. I was standing there, fishing for my library card, when the gift arrived.

"And you know what else is strange?" the librarian said. "Kids come in now, and they walk right past all those Chillers books—and you know what they ask for? You're not going to believe this: *David Copperfield*! We can't keep it on the shelf! I've had to order twenty more copies!"

Ida was right. We knew.